"Give me a chance.
Give *us* a chance...."

Jed hauled Ashley to her feet and backed her against a wall, allowing her no escape. She was breathing hard. Slowly he kissed her eyelashes closed and then captured her mouth.

Ashley moaned. But then she straightened and pushed him away. "Until you can prove I mean more to you than a good time, I'm not interested."

Jed stared while she transformed herself back into the cool, controlled Ashley Jamieson. Suddenly, even in her jeans and sweater, she looked all business. He tried to concentrate on what she was saying.

"Besides, we have more important things to discuss. You do remember why you're here, don't you?"

Jed nodded, mesmerized. She was incredible—warm and wanton one minute, icy and distant the next. And she didn't want anything to do with him. Changing her mind would definitely be a challenge.

He smiled. He loved a challenge....

Hillary Hunter is a Chicago native who now lives in Springfield. She studied film and television in college and did her master's thesis on soap operas. But it wasn't until she stayed up all night—worried because a character on her favorite show was in jail—that she realized just how hooked she was. Hillary admits that she prefers happy endings, though—which is why she decided to write for Harlequin!

COOPER'S LAST STAND

HILLARY HUNTER

Harlequin Books

TORONTO • NEW YORK • LONDON
AMSTERDAM • PARIS • SYDNEY • HAMBURG
STOCKHOLM • ATHENS • TOKYO • MILAN
MADRID • WARSAW • BUDAPEST • AUCKLAND

To Dawn, for being there when I needed her

ISBN 0-373-25596-9

COOPER'S LAST STAND

Copyright © 1994 by Sherry Yanow.

Printed in U.S.A.

Prologue

HER TROUBLE STARTED when the doorbell rang.

Ashley Jamieson jogged through the family room to her apartment door, her stocking feet slapping on the slick hardwood floor. Ignoring the intercom, she buzzed Sean in and opened her door—to empty air and the faint sound of the downstairs street door clicking shut.

Puzzled, Ashley walked to the edge of the landing and peered down. She'd remodeled the first floor of her brownstone into four commercial spaces, and the lobby was deserted, just the way it should have been on a Sunday night. She felt a sudden chill of apprehension as a whiff of fresh October air reached her nose. If it wasn't her brother, Sean, who had she let into her building?

Then she spied something beside the street door. It was a shoe box. A gift-wrapped shoe box. She put her hand to her heart. "Just a package," she muttered. "Nothing to get hysterical about, Jamieson. At least not yet."

Cautiously Ashley walked down the wrought-iron stairway and through the lobby, passing a darkened tailor shop, an orthodontist's office and a financial adviser's. The fourth office was Match-maker, Matchmaker Ltd., the dating service she owned.

With trembling fingers, she picked up the package, noting how carefully the heavy pink paper was folded and taped. She jiggled the box; an object inside slid back and forth.

Ashley cracked open the street door, scanning her cluttered block for anything unusual. She lived on Chicago's Near North Side in an upscale neighborhood. The commercial streets were jammed with restaurants, bars and jazz clubs, and the residential areas were an eclectic mix of brick elevator buildings, brownstones, gothic mansions and glass-box high rises. As she searched her street, Ashley saw only the typical blend of pedestrians and traffic. There was no suspicious beady-eyed character lurking behind the bushes or the wrought-iron fence bordering her small front lawn.

Still, Ashley was frightened. She ran upstairs, awkwardly clutching the box to her side like a football. Setting it on the kitchen's butcher-block table, she tore off the wrapping, gingerly lifted the lid and peeked inside.

"No!" she screamed, frantically pushing the box away.

It teetered on the edge of the table, then a dead canary fell out and dropped to the floor, a note fluttering out of the bird's beak. Hand shaking, Ashley grabbed the scrap of paper, neatly printed with letters cut out of a magazine. It read:

This birdie sings
This birdie's dead
You will be too
Remember what I said

Five minutes later her brother arrived.

Ashley babbled, trying to make herself understood while Sean read the poem.

"It's rhyme number five," she told him, finally forcing herself to calm down.

Sean tossed the note into the shoe box and hugged her close. "Hey, shh. It's okay, Ash. It's okay."

She looked up into Sean's freckled face and felt a tiny bit better. He had always made her feel safe.

Sean pulled back, his kind brown eyes dark with concern. "Now let me get this straight. Rhyme number five?" He stroked his chin. "You mean there are more? Were you ever going to tell me about them, or were you planning to publish them first?"

Ashley tried to laugh, but failed. "They're not very good, Sean. The rest were on my answering machine. I got the first one last week."

Swallowing, she recited the second rhyme:

Hickory dickory dock
Ashley ran up the clock
The clock struck one
And knocked her down
Hickory dickory red
Looks like Ashley's dead

"That does it!" exclaimed Sean. "I'm calling the cops."

"No! And you know why. No police. I don't want—"

Sean held up a hand. "Okay, okay. I'm sorry. I forgot. I know how you feel about cops, so I'll make an appointment with a private investigator for you. I'll call him first thing tomorrow morning. I know just the guy—Megan's cousin used him for her divorce. And I'll pay."

Ashley got as far as opening her mouth to protest.

"Don't even try and argue with me on this. Independence is independence and spunk is spunk, but sick is sick and you need help."

Ashley closed her mouth and nodded. Her brother was right. She'd never had a problem recognizing trouble. And a gift-wrapped dead bird was definitely it. But she wasn't about to let her brother pay for the P.I.

When Sean returned from disposing of the canary, Ashley tossed a salad and finished cooking dinner. She made bright inane conversation, asking all about Megan and the kids, who were visiting Sean's mother-in-law in Florida.

When they sat down to dinner, she ate as if she was starving, although the food tasted like sawdust. Still, she gobbled up every bite and served chocolate-chip ice cream for dessert. She ate that, too, pouring chocolate syrup on top of it. She had to carry on as if everything was normal. She had to stay in control.

After Sean left, Ashley scooped another ball of ice cream onto her plate, coated it with fresh syrup and defiantly spooned ten maraschino cherries on top. "So there," she said to the salt shaker on the table. "Think I'm scared? I'm not. So there," she repeated in a little voice, trying to ignore her stomachache.

Much later, she went to sleep with the bedroom light on, feeling very scared.

1

THE PRIVATE DETECTIVE'S office was in a seedy building on the fringe of the Loop, just half a block from a screeching El. With a sigh, Ashley read the directory in the dilapidated lobby. God, she didn't want to do this! Reluctantly she climbed two creaky stories, dodging flakes of peeling paint. A secretary with yellow hair and an inch of brown roots told her Mr. Anthony was expecting her and pointed a long red fingernail at a door.

Ashley swallowed nervously, not moving. She didn't know what to expect. What did private eyes look like? What did they act like? In frustration, she shoved her fingers through her mass of russet curls. She couldn't believe she was really here. This kind of thing happened in movies, not real life! Who'd want to kill *her*?

She wished she had a mint to suck on; her throat was so dry. *Maybe I'm about to meet the love of my life*, she thought. *Maybe Mr. Anthony'll be a sexy guy in a trench coat and a fedora. Or maybe he'll be like Magnum, P.I.* She shivered, even though the high October sun had warmed her through her cocoa-colored silk suit.

She flinched as the secretary cleared her throat. The woman was staring at her with open curiosity. Ashley knew she couldn't put this off any longer. Taking a giant breath, she pushed open the frosted glass door.

Mr. Anthony was a little man with a Woody Allen face. He wasn't wearing a trench coat, a fedora or anything else remotely romantic. Instead, he wore a white shirt with a string tie, and his feet, propped on his desk, sported pointy lizard-skin boots. His thick glasses had settled on the tip of his nose. Despite her anxiety, Ashley laughed at herself. This guy was no Tom Selleck.

She opened her mouth, intent on a polite ordinary greeting. She wanted to put everything in the hands of the investigator so her life could return to normal.

The detective put his feet on the ground and stood, hand extended. And then a flicker of movement caught Ashley's eye. There was another man in the room. He was struggling to rise from his chair beside the desk. Because of closed venetian blinds, the chair was in shadow, and she couldn't see his face.

The man seemed frozen, half out of his seat. Freeze tag, Ashley thought inanely, remembering the game from her childhood. Then she got a good look at him, and his problem became her problem.

Her hand was suspended in midair, and it wasn't moving. Her mouth hung open in a stupid O. And the strange thing was that even though she couldn't move, her heart was tap-dancing like crazy.

It was him.

Jed Wyatt Cooper—or whatever alias he was using these days—was standing before her in the flesh. And what flesh. His navy T-shirt rippled across his well-muscled chest as he managed to stand, gaping. The navy matched his deep-set eyes. His caramel brown hair was in need of a cut, and the new lines etched around his eyes and mouth gave him a weathered go-to-hell look—a look that would match the wolf-on-the-prowl walk of his.

But Ashley wasn't about to be his prey again. No, she'd learned her lesson well enough the first time. Only one man had ever seen through her cool facade. Jed.

She shuddered. He'd betrayed her once . . .

Exercising a great deal of willpower, Ashley started to breathe again, surreptitiously wiping her hands on her purse. She tried to put enough breaths together to actually speak and break the tableau that had Mr. Anthony nervously eyeing the others. The P.I. slid his glasses back up his nose and coughed.

"Uh, Miss Jamieson..." He clasped her stiff hand. "Take a seat. Meet my associate, Mr. Wyatt." Anthony dashed out from behind his scarred wooden desk, pulling out a chair she thankfully dropped into.

Ashley managed to regain some measure of self-possession and was surprised to notice her body was actually functioning. Her heart still beat. Her blood still flowed. She gave him a weak little smile, starting to relax and beginning to recognize the possibilities. *Maybe this is payback time,* a small voice suggested. *Expose Jed. Tell Mr. Anthony who he really is and exact your revenge.*

"I'm sure we have...a lot of information to share, Mr. Anthony," she said, hesitating, and then warming to the thought. Until now, she'd always considered herself a nice person. The kind of person who delivered hot meals to AIDS victims, took in stray animals and made sandwiches for the homeless. Not until this instant had she realized she might be capable of being...not nice.

Vaguely she was aware that her anxiety was gone, shocked out of her by the sight of Jed Cooper. She directed a steely glare at Jed, who fell back in his chair with a groan. He pushed both hands up through his shaggy hair.

"Just take your time, Miss Jamieson. Gather your thoughts and take your time," Mr. Anthony said kindly, obviously sensing her hesitation, just as obviously mistaking its cause.

Ashley crossed one stocking-clad leg over the other and tossed her long hair back. She was suddenly very clearheaded, fueled by a sizzling rush of adrenaline as she mentally reviewed what she knew about Jed Wyatt Cooper. Jed was *True Life* magazine's star investigative reporter. Obviously the great impostor was here to get a story. She'd learned he worked undercover in one profession after another—as an attorney, soap-opera actor, circus clown, senator's aide, commodities broker, baseball player—and then revealed his pretend life in a series of incisive articles, exposing everything from the glamour to the corruption. Five years ago, Jed had done a piece on dating services, using her newly opened agency as a fertile source of information. She winced. He'd done a superlative job on research.

Ashley leaned forward, convincing herself she owed it to Mr. Anthony to tell him the truth. "Mr. Anthony, I'd like to—" She stopped in midsentence. Jed's eyes held hers in an imploring gaze. God, this was special. Jed Wyatt Cooper actually begging?

Suddenly Ashley knew it wasn't time to expose him, not just yet. She told herself the reason she wasn't going to reveal his secret had nothing whatsoever to do with the vulnerable look in those midnight blue eyes and everything to do with the fact that she was going to make him sweat.

Feeling drunk with revenge, she made a mistake, stealing another look at Jed's eyes. A sharp twinge of remembered passion hit her like a blow. *Those eyes destroyed you,* she reminded herself in self-defense. She shifted in her seat, desperately trying to will the twinge away.

"You first, Mr. Anthony," she demurred. "You're the expert, so I'll defer to you."

Anthony leaned forward, at ease now, perhaps thinking he'd imagined the last awkward few minutes. He tapped a pen on a manila folder and spoke in short bursts. "Well, I had a talk with your brother, Miss Jamieson. He told me about the threatening poems on your answering machine. I bet the perpetrator used spliced tapes to put the rhymes together—random words from TV programs, commercials. He told me about the dead bird, too, and sent over the note and both your prints by messenger. No third-party prints were on it, I'm afraid."

Anthony leaned forward. "Now, even if we knew who the perp was, the phone threats and the bird would only be a misdemeanor charge. And even then, Miss Jamieson, a judge could conceivably order you both to sit down with an arbitrator and work out your problems."

Ashley was shocked. "*Our* problems? Why, that's ridic—"

Anthony waved his hand dismissively. "I know, I know, Miss Jamieson," he said placatingly. "That's why I have another idea. Especially since we don't have a clue as to who the black hat is." Anthony slid a piece of letterhead stationery across the table at her. "Notice my specialties are many. Divorce, surveillance, child custody, courtroom evidence, personal injury. Thirty dollars an hour and expenses. Of course, I don't do it all myself. In fact, I'm due out of town on a missing persons tonight. That's why I have skilled people working for me." He twisted to the side. "Jed Wyatt's your man."

Ashley stifled a snort of derision, settling back in her chair and plastering a bright attentive look on her face.

"He can crack a safe," Anthony was saying, "hot-wire a car, pick a lock, tap a phone, field-strip an M-16. Spent two weeks in Alabama at Pearson's Special Operations Center. Besides being a licensed P.I. and coming to me with excellent references, Wyatt just cracked a baby-selling ring in L.A."

Ashley gritted her teeth, feeling her hard-won self-control starting to slip. She couldn't stand the smug grin Jed got as Anthony sang his praises. Rather than sweating it out, Jed was lounging in the chair, obviously thinking he was home free. He'd tipped back his chair on two legs, looking at her as if he was remembering—in vivid detail—what had happened between them five years ago. Then he winked. The nerve!

Desperately Ashley tried to focus on Mr. Anthony. ". . . at Pearson's, they train counterterrorist agents and presidential bodyguards, among other things. Jed'll ID your stalker, grab him and persuade him to leave you alone *before* the nutbar can hurt you—without a judge getting in the way."

She jabbed a finger at Jed. "Sounds like a plan—as long as *he* isn't involved!"

Jed shot out of his chair, glaring down at her and speaking in the gravelly voice she remembered so well. "It doesn't have to be this way. If you'd listened to me five years—"

"No way, buster!"

"Hey!" Anthony roared. He stood on tiptoe, grabbing Jed by the collar and shoving him in the general direction of his chair. The little P.I. straightened his string tie. "So, you two know each other."

"To my regret—"

"If you'd just let me—"

Anthony banged a brass paperweight down on his desk. "Quiet!" He eyed them both. "Miss Jamieson, you'll let me speak?"

Chagrined, she nodded and bit a nail. She hadn't lost control like this for five years. Being in the same room with Jed made her feel like a live grenade.

The P.I. sat back down, giving a warning look first to Jed, then Ashley. Obediently they both sat. Anthony steepled his fingers. "Now, I don't have another agent to work with you at the moment, Miss Jamieson. So I'd appreciate it if you'd permit me to explain how I'd planned on using Jed before allowing your personal feelings to interfere. I do believe your safety comes first?"

She nodded again, desperately trying to save face and act calm. She was horrified by her outburst. If there was one thing she'd always counted on, it was her ability to stay in control.

"Okay. I wanna send Wyatt in undercover, as a maintenance man in your brownstone. Your brother says there's four offices on the ground floor, your apartment's on the second floor, and it's pretty accessible. And you own the building."

Ashley was intrigued by the sound of the plan, especially when she saw the look of dismay on Jed's rugged face.

"My idea was to offer your current janitor a few months' paid vacation. He's not gonna mind or ask any questions, trust me. Jed moves into the basement apartment and is in the perfect position for surveillance."

"Naturally your agent can fix toilets? Was that part of his training? Repair leaking sinks, tinker with radiators, sweep and vacuum and haul trash? I hope he's good enough to fill Darryl's shoes. Because when I knew him he wasn't very . . . good."

"If he wants to work for me, he'll blend in just fine," Anthony said wearily.

Ashley bit back a mischievous smile, sure that one undercover assignment Jed had never sought was janitor, especially not with her as his boss. Not with his Sears Tower-size ego. Why expose him now? First, she'd see him humbled.

Anthony shifted his gaze to Jed. "Well, Wyatt? Whaddaya think?"

Jed clenched his teeth. "Sure, no problem. Garbageman for a day. Or a week." He shrugged. "Or however long it takes to nab the big bad canary killer." Then his lip quirked upward. "We do know each other, Jack, but it was a long time ago. It was memorable, but hardly important enough to lose my job over."

Ashley forced her lips into a tight smile, hiding her hurt. How could the events of five years ago be just another notch on Jed's belt, when her life had been turned upside down and inside out?

She spoke slowly and carefully as if Jed were a backward child. "Just as long as Jed remembers he has two jobs, Mr. Anthony. As landlord, I like to guarantee my tenants superior service. The orthodontist especially likes his office spick-and-span. Eat-off-the-floor spick-and-span." She tapped her chin. "The basement apartment's not much, but Darryl's never complained. He was just happy to have a job after living at the halfway house. The room's about the size of a postage stamp really."

"About the size of your heart, hmm?"

Anthony threw his hands up into the air. "Cool it, you two. Thirty bucks an hour ain't worth it." He stared at Jed. "Wyatt, can you deal with this or not? This bad guy could be very dangerous. Killing an animal's often only the beginning. You need to comb through Miss Jamieson's entire dating service files for suspects—and if it takes you twenty-four hours a day to do it, you do it. I'm not gonna put a client in jeopardy because of bad feelings. They don't belong on the job, dammit. Can you handle it?" He jammed his glasses high up on his nose.

Jed lowered his eyes. "Yeah, I can handle this," he said through clenched teeth.

"No problem on my end, either," Ashley cooed, comfortably in charge of the situation. "I'm sure Mr. Coo—er, Wyatt will be as good at catching the bad guy as he is at cleaning toilets. Right?"

Jed nodded curtly, a muscle twitching in his cheek.

Ashley got up, hauling her leather purse strap onto her shoulder. "Well, I'll expect you tomorrow at 6 a.m. sharp. It'll take a while to show you the proverbial ropes. Pick up a good toilet brush before you come over." She flashed him a sparkly smile. "See ya."

Languidly she glided out the office. God, vengeance felt good, she told herself, skipping out into the warm autumn sunlight. She tried to ignore the twinge of attraction she still felt for the man. Instead, she decided she hadn't had this much fun since…since Jed had barged into her life five years ago.

And then the twinge became a full-fledged ache. She felt sick and it wasn't because of bad rhyme schemes, too much ice cream or a dead bird.

The memory of the magic she and Jed had shared…and lost, hurt far more.

2

A FINGERNAIL OF SUN was lighting the morning sky when Jed rang Ashley's doorbell, right on time. "Hiya, Jamieson. Gorgeous morning, ain't it?"

A duffel bag was in his hand and that irreverent look was in his eye. He wore a much-washed black T-shirt and jeans that molded his legs indecently. Ashley told herself he could've been an ad for anything to do with pure masculinity. To her dismay, a flash of desire rippled through her body.

Jed threw down his duffel bag. "Be right back, I'm double-parked."

Ashley wiped a wrist across her forehead. He still smelled like wind and lime. The way he had that day he'd swept into her office and her life. She squeezed her eyes shut. It all came back, every last painful detail. . . .

He'd strode into her office and straddled a chair backward. He proceeded to tell her that he was an attorney with legal aid, uptown branch and that he was a lonely guy who handled ninety-six cases a week and was lucky to get two hours' sleep on his office couch.

"All my time's taken up with depositions or briefs. A lady would be much prettier." He picked out a handful of red jelly beans from the jar on the coffee table and popped them into his mouth.

Trying not to stare, she gave Jed her introductory talk by rote. "Well, Mr. Wyatt, maybe I can help you. If you'll fill out my questionnaire, which includes basic things like height, weight and whether you smoke, and then tell me about your interests . . ."

Jed leaned over the table, staring at her bare ring finger. He crumbled the questionnaire into a ball, tossing it into the wastebasket. "Miss Jamieson, may I call you Ashley?"

Not bothering to wait for permission, he continued. "Let me just tell you what I'm looking for, Ashley. I like petite women, about—" he cocked his head "—five one, with heart-shaped faces and hair the color of falling leaves and eyes that show every emotion. And I like—" he leaned closer still, forcing her to lean back "—surprise, interest and challenge."

He shoved his hands into his pockets and smiled a lazy smile that showed off a dimple. "That's what I look for in a woman."

She shifted in the creaky rocker. "Mr. Wyatt, I make it a policy never to date a client."

"Why?"

"Why? Well, because . . ." And then she couldn't think of one damn reason.

She shivered, stubbornly trying to resist the mysterious pull of this forthright male who was picking out another handful of her favorite red candies.

She slapped down another questionnaire. "Fill out the questionnaire, Mr. Wyatt. I will not call you Jed, because we do not know each other. And we will not know each other in the future, except on a professional basis. Leave me your photo or have one taken and drop it off. I'll see what I can do."

She gave him a dismissive look, one that never failed to put men—from CEOs to truck drivers—in their place. "Men like you have to exercise patience, Mr. Wyatt. Women can't be ordered like hamburger."

"Medium rare."

"Pardon me?"

"I like my hamburgers medium rare." He crumbled the new questionnaire and tossed it into the wastebasket as accurately as the first. "But it's not a piece of meat I want. It's a gorgeous day outside. It's a day to celebrate."

She was in complete agreement. But she had her policies, and she wasn't about to . . .

His eyes darkened, and he tensed like a cat, reading her face. "Hell. You know I'm right."

In an instant, he reached for her arm and was urging her out of her chair. He scanned her open appointment book, a shaggy lock of hair falling over his forehead. "You're free for the rest of the afternoon. Come on, we'll walk to the Lincoln Park Zoo. We can laugh at the traffic backed up on Fullerton—all those sad people stuck in their cars on a day like this. We can do anything. We can even smell the lilacs."

Lilacs. She inched back against the wall, appalled and eager at the same time. "Why?" she managed. "Do you have relatives at the zoo? Like the gorillas?" She looked significantly at his hand on her arm.

He laughed, then dropped his hand. "Come on. Since when is a sassy redhead afraid of a little challenge? Come take a walk through the zoo with me and tell me how Ashley Jamieson got into the dating game and all about your most interesting clients." He held his hands up. "I'm really as harmless as a puppy. Honest."

He dug into his pocket and carelessly tossed $400 onto the table. "There—$200 every six months, paid up one year in advance. And I get you as a bonus. What do you think?"

She didn't, couldn't move. *Smell the lilacs*, he'd said. Of all the flowers to choose . . .

Jed lost the grin and stared at her. He spoke earnestly, his eyes strangely dark again, as if seeing something unexpected. "Please, Ashley. Let me take you to the zoo. You won't regret it. I promise to be good." His voice was husky and dangerously persuasive. "I know you want to go."

And that was how it began. She'd sold her body, her soul and her heart for a few lines from a charming con man.

Ashley's eyes snapped open at the sound of Jed's tuneless whistle. As he sauntered through the wrought-iron gate, she turned her back on him before he could see how unsettled she was.

"Follow me," she said over her shoulder, and led Jed under the brownstone's stone archway and into the foyer of the marvelous old building.

Sunlight filtered in through the floor-to-ceiling casement windows she'd installed. And a two-story diagonal window illuminated the spiral staircase to her apartment. She'd had enough dark times in her life; she craved the sun and things that bloomed.

Putting a tight rein on his emotions, Jed reminded himself his business with Ashley was strictly professional. He would pretend to be her janitor—if that's what she wanted—while he looked for the creep who was bothering her. Because despite what she thought, he was a damn good P.I.

He noted the layout of the building as they strode through the brownstone, taking in the elegant stained-glass doors opening into each rental space—Ashley's and the orthodontist's offices facing east, the tailor's and financial adviser's offices opening west. Just as he remembered.

He studied every inch of the foyer and the floor above. A twisting, wrought-iron stairway led to Ashley's apartment. There was a fire escape in back, he recalled. The whole setup was an invitation for trouble. For all her city ways, Ashley was as trusting as a country girl. This place was wide open and full of windows—easy pickings for a wacko. It would be like shooting goldfish in a bowl.

Jed's eyes narrowed. There wasn't a lot a security system could do. Ashley couldn't very well block the public's access to the four businesses. And he didn't think she'd want to install a heavy door on her apartment. To catch the creep, he was going to have to rely on his ingenuity.

Ashley spoke to Jed over her shoulder as they left the foyer and descended the stairs into a dingy concrete basement with no charm whatsoever. She'd seen him checking windows, entrances, exits. At least he was doing his job. "Your new living quarters," she said, stopping in front of a small room and pushing open the door. "I do hope everything is suitable." She gestured. "The boiler room's the other way, across from the sheds and storage area."

Jed tossed his duffel bag onto the bed, breathing in Ashley's heady scent. Helplessly he could feel the tight rein he'd put on his feelings begin to loosen.

He'd known a lot of women, but Ashley was different. And now the one woman who'd been more than a meaningless conquest was back in his life and driving him crazy. She'd toyed with him in Anthony's office as if the magic they'd made five years ago was worthless. And he had a feeling she wasn't done with him yet.

He sighed heavily. "I've been in worse places."

Rubbing a hand over his jaw, Jed eyed the sagging cot. It wouldn't be long enough for his six feet three inches. The stuffing was seeping out of an ugly chair, and the couch was Herculon tweed, sturdy enough to survive an earthquake.

He moved to the tiny bathroom and groaned. A claw-foot tub with a hand-held shower head took up most of its space. The tub was obviously not meant for anyone over five feet tall. Jed ducked his head out of the bathroom door. "Where do the grown-ups bathe?"

She looked down, smothering a smile, and then pointed out the studio apartment's open door. "Darryl's cleaning cart. Keep a list of what supplies are nearly empty. Floors washed three times a week. Make sure toilets are cleaned every morning and that there's a fresh supply of toilet paper and paper towels. And watch out for Helen, the orthodontist's office manager. She eats up janitors and spits them out. After you get your work done, you can meet me in my office and I'll give you my files to look through. See if you can find a disgruntled client who wants to do me in."

She arranged her features into a mask, not letting him see how he was affecting her.

Jed grinned wickedly. "Disgruntled? With you? Not a snowball's chance in a microwave."

Hands on hips, feet apart, Jed sucked in a breath and looked Ashley over. Her wide-set eyes mirrored her every thought. Thoughts that said she hated his being here, hated him for looking at her. Such a delicate little nose, nostrils flaring with indignation. And her skin, the cream color of a natural redhead with none of the freckles, was pinkening with heat.

Jed damned his own body for wanting more than a look. He shifted uncomfortably, licking his lips. They could have something together if only she'd listen to him, listen and forgive. He could understand where the anger was coming from, but if she'd just let him explain, they could rekindle the fire they'd once made. Jed dragged a hand through his hair, determined to try to reach Ashley, even if it was only for a fleeting reunion.

"Jamieson, listen to me. Let me explain. Please."

She didn't pretend not to know what he meant. She was never good at lies. "Any explaining you're going to do is going to be to your boss—after I tell him you're a cheat and a liar. Can't you be charged with fraud for doing this?"

Jed looked deep into her eyes, hoping to see at least a glimmer of desire. He flinched. What he saw was hurt and anger and betrayal, as if it had all happened yesterday.

He dropped to the thin cot and lay back against the wall, hands folded behind his head, speaking in a weary voice. "It's not fraud, Jamieson. I always have all the qualifications I need, and I always do my job. I pass courses, I get certified. I admit my publisher occasionally pulls strings to cut through red tape. But I'm everything Anthony said I was. I've never been a bodyguard, but I've done divorce work in Little Rock, trailed a fugitive in Portland, solved a missing persons in Scarsdale. And I did work on the baby-selling case in L.A. I'm good. And if I decide to write about my adventures there's no crime in that. In the end people either welcome the publicity or quietly accept it. Suing would just make it more public. And if I expose some wrongdoing along the way, that's in the public's interest.

"And, Ashley? This job's on the house. I'll pay Anthony."

"Ha! I suppose that makes everything all right."

Jed shot upright. She was going to know the truth if he had to tie her up so she'd listen. "I'm also an attorney, Jamieson," he hurried on, not giving her a chance to bolt. "I'm truly sorry I hurt you, Ashley. I never wanted to do that. But listen to me. *Everything* I told you five years ago was true. At least, it was true then, except—"

"Except you're also a user," she snarled. "A liar. Plan to seduce Mr. Anthony, too? Or maybe his secretary?"

"Not my type. Neither of 'em."

"Oh, spare me. *I'm* your type, right? Well, it takes two, Wyatt. Or should I say Cooper?"

"Why, Jamieson? If you hate me so much, why haven't you said anything?"

"Maybe I like making you sweat. Maybe I'll say something . . . and maybe I won't. And maybe because I like seeing you do an honest day's work for a change. Real work. Something besides seducing naive young women. Because that's what you're so good at, isn't it? Taking advantage of young women? Stealing their innocence? By the way, I've seen both, and I think your bedroom technique is far better than your writing!"

She took grim satisfaction in seeing Jed recoil as if he'd been slapped. "So, not another word about five years ago, Cooper. It was a lifetime ago. Understand?" She sucked in a deep breath. "Here." She threw a pair of denim coveralls at him. "Get into these and I'll introduce you to Mr. Salerno, the tailor. He opens at seven."

SHE WAITED for him in the lobby.

The memories crowded her as she sat on a wooden bench. She leaned her head against the cool marble wall, helpless to prevent the onslaught of the past....

She and Jed had enjoyed a sun-filled day at the zoo. A crazy wonderful day watching monkeys and tigers, and talking about movies, musicals and the best hot-dog stands in Chicago.

They had dinner at Stephano's, a cozy restaurant nestled under the rumbling El. She asked him about himself.

He protested at first. "Aw, you don't want me to bore you...."

"I'm not bored. Honest. I want to know all about the man who can work for the downtrodden and pick up the unpickupable all in the same day."

His eyebrow quirked. "Unpickupable?"

"Yeah. It's just not done. Not with me, at least. So you owe me. Now talk."

He rubbed a finger around the rim of his wineglass. "Only if you take a turn later." A corner of his mouth twisted. "I have a feeling that you're far more interesting."

"Okay." She tapped his hand with a spoon. "But it's your turn first. So talk. About you."

He did. He'd been raised in New York. His father was a senior partner in a prestigious Manhattan law firm that specialized in forming partnerships to buy out struggling companies.

"The best in his field," Jed said curtly, fingers gripping his wineglass tightly. She didn't think he even noticed; he was focused too intently on his father. "He planned on me joining, too."

Jed chuckled. "But I discovered I didn't want it, Ash, despite the fact that I was very much my father's son. My mother died when I . . . she died a long time ago. I was shuttled off to prep school, but Father was there for me—for every play, every debate, every football game. I went to Cornell and Northwestern, just like he did. But I found my heart wasn't in mergers and acquisitions and deals."

Jed's voice softened. "I discovered I wanted to help battered women. And the foster parents who wanted to adopt their wards, only to be blocked by a stupid bureaucracy that didn't take the kid's welfare into consideration at all."

He'd searched her face as she felt it drain of color, remembering. "Hey, you okay?"

She gulped. "Yeah, I'm okay. Go on, please."

He traced aimless patterns on the tablecloth with his fork. "In law school I worked for the university's legal clinic and for legal aid, where I am now. Some of those attorneys worked 110 hours a week in leaky offices with taped-over light switches and drafty waiting rooms."

He smiled sheepishly. "Hey, maybe I can't make the world better—I'm no starry-eyed idealist. But if I can change even one person's life, that's what counts. Every person deserves the best legal representation possible in court, rich or poor."

She took a long look at him. "Then it's lucky there are lawyers like you, Jed. For the kids...and, well, for whoever needs it."

And then she confided in him, half surprising herself by keeping her promise to talk. "In lots of ways I'm kind of the opposite to you. I tread carefully. And my life's structured, organized. I like it that way. I kind of let the city be my excitement."

Her eyes lit up. "I am good at what I do, though. I get definite satisfaction out of making a difference in someone's life, too. In my own way."

Ashley went on and on, telling Jed how she got her agency started with a degree from the University of Illinois in interpersonal communications and a small trust fund. "When I graduated, all I knew was that I wanted to stay in Chicago to be near my brother Sean. I'd practically been running a dating service for my college friends, anyway, so it wasn't taking that big of a jump. After I renovated the brownstone, I started advertising—the Yellow Pages, the *Chicago Reader*, a few radio and late-night television spots. I even went to singles meetings like Parents without Partners and passed out my card."

She shrugged. "Now, of course, a lot of my business is by word of mouth."

Encouraged by the interest in Jed's eyes, Ashley told him how she talked her clients through their fears of the dreaded first date and the cute tales about their courtship. She laughed wryly. "Sometimes it's crazy, like when the guy calls to tell me her answering machine plays Barry Manilow, and he despises Barry Manilow. Or that she should lose ten pounds. And then the woman tells me he wouldn't share his popcorn, and she loathes his mustache. But then I think about how many weddings I've been invited to and—"

Jed leaned forward. "Have you ever thought maybe you get more pleasure out of your clients' relationships than you do your own? It's the same thing as standing back and letting the city be your excitement. Ashley Jamieson, you're a voyeur."

She could feel her face flame, instantly humiliated by his deadly accurate reading of her. "I don't appreciate your . . . your curbside psychoanalysis," she sputtered. "And I am, uh, was involved with a wonderful man, a brilliant archaeologist. We just broke up after two years of—"

"Being safe and boring. Don't even bother to deny it. And whoever this fairly safe and boring guy was, his memory didn't stop you from coming out with me today. And it's not going to stop me from—" he caught her hand in his and raised it to his lips "—this."

She thought her body ignited when his lips brushed her flesh. He seemed to know her better than she did herself. His perceptive eyes were kind and caring—and full of desire.

Remarkably she confessed more. She told him the untellable—about her parents and about afterward. She told him things she'd never even told Sean, things she'd kept deep inside.

Her voice finally dwindled away. She shifted her eyes and intently studied the purple light fixture.

"Hey, Ashley, come back to me." He still held her hand and was gently rubbing it across his lips. He leaned forward until their noses nearly touched.

"Honey, you have more resilience in this little finger—" he kissed it "—than I do in my whole body. I think you're terrific. You survived. Now you just have to live."

Ashley saw a pulse tattoo his cheek and suddenly she wasn't embarrassed anymore. She saw herself with his eyes, and astonishingly, what she saw made her feel good. Very good and very desirable.

And then she'd wondered what was going to happen next. . . .

3

THE CLEANING CART rumbled on the tiled lobby floor, stopping abruptly next to her. Ashley jumped and looked up. She saw Jed lounging against the wall, wearing a uniform several sizes too small. He didn't say a word.

She cleared her throat. "Follow me," she said in a small voice.

Ashley led the way to the tailor's, holding the door open and wincing at the look on Jed's face. He was wrapped in a quiet coldness, his lips drawn into a razor-thin line.

She blinked at a ludicrous thought. It was as if she'd hurt him. But she quickly convinced herself that was nonsense. Although she had to admit—if only to herself—that she'd been a very willing partner five years ago.

She moved toward the straw-thin tailor who was busy behind the counter. "Tony, this is Jed. He'll be taking over for Darryl for a while. You can get him started right away."

"Sure, sure," Tony said, smoothing his mustache and looking through the day's orders. "You can sweep, Jed," he said in his accented English. "Always I need sweeping for straight pins, thread, fabric . . ."

"Tony, pssst." Ashley spoke to the tailor in a stage whisper while Jed started sweeping. She was determined to tease some sort of human reaction out of him. Even if it meant going to extremes.

"Keep an eye on him, Tony," she whispered loudly. "Jed's here from the halfway house. On parole for fraud. He meets women through lonely-hearts clubs, promises them the moon, then defrauds them of their life's savings. Older women. Well, you know." The broom thumped louder and louder each time it came down on the floor. The back of Jed's neck was a dull red.

"Ashley, you take care of yourself," Tony said, looking at Jed dubiously. "This world's not a safe place."

"Oh, I'm perfectly safe, Tony. I have Jed's parole officer's name and number. One wrong move, and he's back in prison. He's absolutely harmless." She babbled on as Tony stepped into the back room, arms loaded with clothes. She knew the tailor wouldn't be able to hear her from there, but with his back to them both, Jed didn't know that.

"Perfectly harmless," she warbled. "Good with sweet talk, but apparently all talk, no action. That's how he got turned in. Couldn't, um, satisfy his marks, you know?"

The broom crashed to the floor. Jed spun around and strode toward her. Her trick had worked—the blank frozen look was gone. Instead, the narrowed dark eyes were glinting with indignation. She smothered a little shriek as he bore down on her. Jed stopped abruptly at the cleaning cart, just as she backed hard into the wall.

Jed gathered an armful of supplies. "I'll clean your bathroom now, Mr. Salerno," he called out calmly. "Then I'll be out of your way before any customers arrive." He lowered his voice into a throaty caress. "If that's okay with you, Ms. Jamieson."

She saw the muscle jump in his cheek. She'd gotten rid of his cold dead look only to have it replaced by another, hotter one, laced with all sorts of promise. She gulped. "Yes. Fine. You, uh, finish up here and then meet me in my office as we discussed."

Heart beating like a sparrow's, she ducked out the door. As she unlocked her office and ducked into her private bathroom, she wondered what was happening to her. For the next five minutes all she did was sit on the closed toilet seat, forehead dropped into her palms. "I hate him I hate him I hate him," she moaned, not sure if she was reminding herself or convincing herself.

After lashing cold water on her face, she braced her hands on the counter, steadying her shaky body. The face in the mirror was a fright, skin as white as cream cheese, eyes as big as a deer's. She shook her head. If the stalker's goal was to make her life miserable and confuse her beyond belief, he was succeeding brilliantly.

But she wasn't about to concede defeat just yet. Throwing back her shoulders, she sailed into her office, intent on metamorphosing back into sane practical Ashley Jamieson.

She jumped a foot when something touched her shoulder.

"What's wrong, Ash? A little nervous?"

She released a deep breath. "Don't sneak up on me like that, Sean. Especially not now, not with everything . . ."

He nodded, his carrot hair flopping over his forehead. "You're right. I'm sorry, kid. I just saw the open door. I didn't think about what's been going on or anything." He cleared his throat. "But we need to talk about something else."

Sean looked apologetic. She knew she couldn't be mad at him; it would be like being mad at a teddy bear. She plopped into her comfortable rocker. Sean didn't just drive an hour from his Barrington home for the second time in four days for a social visit. She popped a jelly bean into her mouth, wondering what was coming.

Sean smiled gently. "Hey, you look beat. Tell me all about Mr. Anthony after I get you a cup of coffee." Sean busied himself at the coffeemaker, soothing her with meaningless chatter while they waited for the coffee.

He set her mug on the distressed-wood coffee table, which was littered with skookum American Indian dolls—souvenirs made for tourists in the early part of the century. There were Indian accents in every corner, from a kilim-covered mirror to a totem-pole coatrack. Their parents had owned an antique shop specializing in Indian artifacts, and Ashley had taken everything out of storage when she bought the brownstone. A diamond-patterned love seat, a match to the two in Ashley's apartment, was backed up against a long slate table. On the table were a photo of Ashley's kitten Smoky, a collection of antique clocks and a brass tortoise. There was no desk; the office might've been a comfortable family room.

Sean settled into the love seat, and Ashley began a detailed explanation about Mr. Anthony and how she came to have an undercover janitor. She stopped in the middle of a sentence. "Oh, here he is now," she said, her body stiffening, "my very own janitor-detective." Composing herself, she waved an arm, speaking evenly and determined to control the situation. "Jed, this is my brother, Sean. He's the one who insisted on calling in a P.I."

Sean, at five eight, only came up to Jed's chin as they shook hands and exchanged pleasantries. Coolly, Ashley instructed Jed to gather the files together and meet her at her apartment in an hour.

Jed gave her an irreverent salute in return. "Don't mind me, Ms. Ashley, I'll be back scrubbing toilets in a jiff." He winked, then dropped to his knees in front of the file cabinets in a far corner of the office and started pulling out folders.

Feeling neither cool nor in control, Ashley darted a look at her watch, ignoring Sean's amused expression. "Uh, I'm really sorry, Sean, but my first client's due in ten minutes." She gestured toward the large casement window as if her client could be seen coming down the street with the swarm of others in the busy rush hour. At that moment came the punch of a jackhammer from a construction crew, drowning out the sounds of traffic.

"I have to accommodate people's schedules," Ashley said, raising her voice over the din. "It isn't easy." She sat up straight and threw Sean a bright smile. "So, what can I do for you?"

Sean shifted his gaze to Jed and lowered his voice. "It's about Stephen."

Stephen!

Ashley rocked back so far she almost tipped the chair over. "Stephen?" she squeaked. "He's on a dig. What can you—"

"The poor guy called me. Very long distance. You know we got friendly after he started coming to me for dental work? I did that bridge and those root canals and—"

"Sean . . ."

"Well, anyway, your professor's coming back from the Jordan Valley soon, and he wants to know if he's got any chance with you at all. Even for a patient man, seven years is a long time, Ashley."

Ashley turned the color of a bad sunburn, knowing that Jed was in the corner of the large office busily flipping through folders. Too far away to hear them, she told herself.

She leaned closer to Sean and whispered, "Stephen thinks I'm going to fall in love with him, and he won't take no for an answer. Even when I broke up with him five years ago, he came back and insinuated himself into my life all over again. And I *do* have strong feelings for him. It's just not love."

Sean gave her a shrewd look. "Ashley, I think you're making a mistake. I told Stephen I couldn't speak for you but that I'd speak *to* you." He gave her a crooked grin. "I really like the guy. And I've never met anybody more persistent."

She shook her head, glancing at Jed, whose head was bent in what seemed like serious study.

"Ashley, I'm saying this for your own good, and I think it's something Dad would've said to you. I want you to take a long hard look at you and Stephen. I care about you too much to see you throw away a good relationship."

She was caught in a swirl of crazy emotions, forcing herself to confront things she rarely let herself feel, let alone analyze.

"And where does love come in, Sean? You haven't mentioned it once. Like your love for Megan? Love and—" her eyes shifted to Jed's stiff shoulders again "—p-passion." God, what was she saying? True love and passion were for her clients. She'd thought she was beyond that—thanks to her disastrous encounter with Jed. What was happening to her?

Sean's fair skin took on the color of his hair. He rubbed the back of his neck. "Ashley, uh, maybe you haven't given the guy a chance. I mean . . ."

Ashley tried to freeze the mischievous smile twitching her lips. Sometimes she thought Sean had frozen her in time—she'd be his fourteen-year-old kid sister for life.

"I do know all about the birds and the bees, Sean. And shouldn't I think of Stephen as, um—" Ashley cleared her throat "—exciting? I mean, I've never exactly discussed it with him, but he knows my feelings don't match his and still, he won't let go. The chemistry just isn't there."

Sean bit his lip. "Well, okay. Except... Hell, this is hard to say, but maybe you need to give Stephen a chance to kindle the kind of passion you want. Granted, it's been seven years, but if you haven't honestly given the guy a chance, twenty years couldn't do it. I can't believe I'm saying this, but wear something slinky and go out for a romantic evening with the guy and give him a chance to show you this passion."

A file drawer crashed shut, the metal cabinets trembling with the vibration. "Uh, sorry," Jed muttered from his corner, getting up with his arms loaded with folders. "I'll take this first set of files down to my place, put 'em in some sort of order and then meet you later, boss."

Noisily Jed kicked all the other file drawers closed and finally left, slamming the office door shut so hard the pane of stained glass rattled.

"Moody guy," Sean said as the rattle subsided. "He definitely looks capable. Actually, when he charged out of here, he looked lethal." Sean shook his head. "Anyway, sis, give Stephen a chance. Maybe something will happen between you two. Anything that's lasted for seven years deserves one final chance. Right?"

She plastered a smile on her face. "Sure, you're right. And thanks for coming." Ashley hugged her brother. "Thanks for caring."

After her brother left, Ashley settled herself deep into the oak rocker, checking her watch. Amanda Bergman, her first appointment, was always late.

With a sigh, she steepled her fingers, forcing herself to think about what Sean had said. It was true that Stephen was a great guy. Reliable, sincere, trustworthy. *Yeah, and so is a Saint Bernard,* said an impish voice. She bit her lip, telling herself that giving Stephen one last chance might not be a bad idea.

"In fact, maybe a life with Stephen's just what I need," she murmured, rocking gently back and forth. "Marriage, a home in the suburbs, a minivan and lots of studious little children. Maybe it would complete my life."

A life, she mused, that had only seemed complete once—that day and night she'd spent with Jed. The night, especially the night. Ashley felt her heart do a little flip at the memory....

Jed had brought her home after dinner. He braced his hands on the carved doorframe above her head, looking down at her. "Ash, today has meant a lot to me. More than you can know. If you feel the way I do, it can mean a whole lot more."

His searching eyes were filled with desire. Ashley stood on tiptoe and brushed back a stray lock of hair from his forehead. He looked all male—hungry male. And yet, she knew she had total control over him. She'd never felt more powerful, desirable, exciting.

He dragged his fingers through her hair. "It's so soft, so wonderful."

"No, it's frizzy and wild and unmanageable."

He buried his nose in her curls and whispered, "Shut up, Jamieson. It's gorgeous. *You're* gorgeous."

He angled his mouth over hers, nibbling on her lower lip and caressing it with his tongue, asking silently for more. Shyly she opened her mouth to him.

As the kiss deepened, her bones and muscles melted. Jed finally pulled away, rubbing the pad of his thumb across her lower lip. "I swear I'll make it good for you."

She wasn't very experienced. In fact, she'd never made love before. Safe bland Stephen was the only other man she'd dated, and he was nothing like Jed. When Jed unbuttoned her silk blouse he nibbled the skin revealed until she tingled. He danced her backward to the couch, easing her blouse off her shoulders and seeding her breasts with kisses. Throwing back her head, Ashley closed her eyes and moaned, not quite sure what was happening to her. She only knew she didn't want it to stop.

"Oh, honey," Jed crooned, unsnapping her bra and tossing it aside. Then his lips found her nipples and he tenderly teased them into hard nubs with his teeth.

Hot and dazed, Ashley sagged against him. He lowered her onto the couch, then a smile tugged at his lips. "You know what happens to bewitchingly beautiful women who can't stand up but still want more?"

"W-what?"

"This." Jed unzipped her long skirt, his big hands sliding over the silk and peeling it off. Then he dropped to his knees beside the couch and kissed her through her lace panties.

Ashley trembled. Something was happening to her. Something . . . She shuddered. Gently Jed parted her thighs and his tongue flicked at her core through the silk. Ashley whimpered, suddenly afraid of these new feelings.

"Ashley, let it happen," Jed crooned. With one smooth motion, he removed the scrap of silk.

Shocked, Ashley realized she was wet, very wet. Jed drank from her.

"No, I . . ." She moaned, embarrassed. Embarrassed yet feeling she'd just found a little piece of heaven.

"Should I stop?"

Liquid fire pulsed through her veins. The ache and need inside her was unbearable. "No. No. Don't stop. Oh..." She arched her back, almost out of control.

Jed stroked her with one finger, then two fingers, all the while crooning her name, and her embarrassment faded. She let go, riding hot rhythmic waves of honey.

The tremors faded, and she rested, trying to control her breathing. Still on his knees, Jed nestled his head between her breasts. Ashley stirred, and he raised his head.

"Oh!" Her hand flew to her mouth. "You're not even... your clothes..."

Jed's lips quirked into a desire-filled smile. "Honey, that was just prep school. Are you ready for some higher education?"

Ashley's eyes glittered, accepting his challenge. She rose to her knees, taller than he was for a change, and slowly unbuttoned Jed's shirt. She shucked it off, surprised at her boldness. "I'm a good student, Jed."

He laughed softly, his eyes dark and gleaming.

"No," she whispered. "No laughing in this class. I'm very, very strict with my teachers. I expect a lot."

Sinuously Ashley moved against him and rubbed her breasts against his muscular chest. She felt him go taut, heard him suck in a breath. Following instincts she'd never known she had, she clasped Jed's hands, motioning him up.

"Now, it's my turn," she murmured. Not quite sure she wasn't possessed by some otherworldly force, Ashley unbuckled Jed's belt and unzipped his pants as a strong erotic pulse beat within her.

Was she doing it right? Was this seduction? Her heart hammering, she pulled off Jed's slacks and briefs, her fingers gliding lightly over his washboard stomach, his lean hips, his . . .
She swallowed.

Jed trembled at every touch of her hands. He wasn't laughing anymore. He was simply letting her do with him what she would.

Ashley pressed her head against Jed's crinkled mat of hair. "Am I doing it right, teach?"

He groaned. "Doing it right?" he said in a strangled voice. "It's all I can do not to take you here on the couch." Bending over, he took a foil packet out of his pants' pocket. He swept Ashley up in his arms and carried her off to her big brass bed.

Above her Jed was all hard planes and muscle and . . . She gulped, her eyes lowering to what she hadn't looked at before. He was magnificent.

Jed followed her eyes. "Do you trust me, honey?"

She swallowed, nodding, her newfound boldness gone.

Jed raised her hands over her head. He swayed over her sensuously, brushing his length between her thighs and across her belly, stroking until she became as moist as before.

Stunned, Ashley realized it was happening all over again. She moaned.

Jed slowed, his eyes knowing. He let go of her hands, taking a second to slide on the condom, then she was back in his arms.

He entered her slowly, filling her until she thought she'd scream with the want. Even the small first-time hurt didn't diminish it, although she let out a soft gasp.

He tensed. "Did I hurt you, honey?"

"No, oh, no. Don't stop." She gripped him tighter, crossing her ankles over his hips. "Don't ever stop."

"Is that an order?"

"Yes."

An amused light in his eye, Jed rocked inside her, burying himself deeply. He thrust gently, letting her adjust and holding back with a groan. "Let me know when you want more."

Ashley whimpered for more.

Cupping her bottom with both hands, Jed plunged deeper.

"Yes," she breathed. "Oh, yes." This was what she'd been waiting for.

Jed's eyes darkened, and he increased the pace until everything exploded. Frantically Ashley dug her fingers into Jed's back. She moaned his name while he encouraged her, praised her. And then he groaned, climaxing deep inside her.

Afterward, Ashley lay quietly, wrapped snugly in Jed's arms.

"Was it good?" he asked.

"It was more than good." She sighed. "I, um, can see doing this again. One day."

Jed's lip twitched. "Oh, you will, honey. That's a promise. Maybe before one day."

It had definitely been more than good, Ashley thought. So much better than anything she'd ever imagined. That was her last thought before she fell asleep in the warmth of his arms.

In the morning, Jed woke her with a kiss and a whisper. "Jamie . . ." he murmured, sending a stir through her loins at the diminutive of her last name. That husky voice made her shiver. "Jamie, I have to fly to New York this morning about, um, a client."

He drew her to his muscled chest, his long fingers playing with her thick hair. "I'll be back in two days, and then we're going to begin this relationship for real."

He rubbed his cheek against hers, his stubble scratching. "Jamie, I have things to tell you. Things about my past . . ."

She shook her head, trusting him. Consciously going against every lesson she'd painfully learned since she was fourteen. "No, Jed, I don't think we're about the past. What's important is now. Come back to me soon," she whispered, her small hands bringing his head down so that his lips were on her mouth.

"Jamie," he groaned. "I think I've got to keep that promise I made last night. About before one day..."

God, is this what love felt like?

Her happiness lasted twenty-four hours. She was reading the *National Daily* the next morning when she found the article. It was a small piece, buried in the business section. An interview with Jed Wyatt Cooper, the Great Impostor, telling about his latest exposé—this time he was blowing the cover off dating services.

She was waiting for him at the door after he called to say he'd landed at O'Hare and would be over soon. Before he said a word, she'd smacked him with the newspaper. "The Great Impostor, indeed. Aptly named." Then she slapped his face with her hand. Once. Twice. When she tried to slap him a third time he grabbed her wrist.

"Goddammit, Ashley, listen to me! I can explain. Everything I said was true! Everything except—"

"Except you cleverly didn't say, 'Ashley, I'm doing undercover work, tell me all your secrets and go to bed with me for dessert.' Well, you can go to hell!"

He left after she threw two glass paperweights at his head. He phoned every day, and she hung up on him. He sent roses, candy, stuffed animals and lilacs. She threw it all in the garbage. On the fifth day, she finally spoke to Jed, inviting him over.

She met him at the door with an attack dog she'd rented. "Max, guard!" she ordered. One hundred and thirty pounds of snarling rottweiler pinned Jed to the wall.

"Now do you understand that I never want to see you again, Jed Wyatt Cooper? You make me sick. I want you gone. By the way, the word after 'guard' is a-t-t-a-c-k." She spelled it out very slowly.

Jed looked at her in disbelief. "You wouldn't!"

"Oh, wouldn't I! Just try me. Get lost, Jed. Get lost where you can't be found. I mean it."

His eyes narrowed. "You are the most unreasonable, stubborn, infuriating woman I have ever—"

"Max, a—"

"Okay, you win." Face white, Jed left.

And silently, she watched him go.

She told herself he'd stolen her innocence.

He'd betrayed her trust.

She told herself she hated him.

And then she asked herself why the people she loved always left her.

ASHLEY TRUDGED up to her apartment. Her meeting with Amanda Bergman had taken well over the customary forty-five minutes. Which wasn't unusual with the fickle Amanda, even though the process of a match couldn't be simpler.

Ashley had offered Amanda three carefully selected potential dates, showing her a picture and giving her a detailed summary of each man's personal questionnaire. As well, Ashley had offered her own opinion based on her personal interview with each client. Ashley was convinced the personal touch was superior to videos and soulless computers.

Today, Amanda had chosen Brent Kelly, a radio news director. Next, Ashley would show Brent Amanda's picture and summary. If Brent was interested, he'd call.

Ashley paused at a step, amused. The guys *always* wanted to meet Amanda, a five-foot-ten fashion model and Vanna White-type. Brent would probably call her from the first available phone.

The men usually went for looks, Ashley thought wryly, the women for status. Sometimes, even a minor point in a client's file made a difference. Like the woman who'd used an office photo of herself and was never chosen until Ashley suggested she have a more casual picture taken in her backyard. After that the woman was chosen regularly.

"Amanda, though," Ashley muttered. "Amanda's got to be difficult." Sometimes Amanda demanded six clients to choose from. And if none struck her fancy, she'd ask for six more.

"Thank goodness, she was happy today," Ashley said to herself. "Or you'd have to offer her Jed."

Ashley chuckled humorlessly.

Weary, she rested at the landing. She dropped her head and then flung it back until her hair touched her waist. She felt like taking a nap that would last about a year. Maybe she'd wake up in a new world, all her troubles gone. Like Dorothy, over the rainbow and into a brand-new life.

She continued toward her apartment, then stopped dead, pulled rudely from her daydream. Her door was swinging open, and the intricate beveled-glass insert was in jagged pieces on the tile floor.

No!

Tentatively stepping inside the apartment, Ashley stood still, her mouth open. And then she tried to scream, but a big hand clapped itself over her mouth, choking off her cry.

Struggling against a hard male chest, Ashley bit the hand as hard as she could. She tasted blood and heard a muffled curse before she fainted.

4

"Ashley, it's me!"

Jed whirled her around to face him, his hands gripping her shoulders. "I'm sorry if I hurt you," he said as she came to. "I didn't want you to scream and scare the wits out of everyone in the building."

She was staring up at him, a weak helpless look in her eyes. Dammit, he wished he could've spared her this.

The family room had been ransacked. Before he could touch a thing he'd had to wait for Anthony's evidence technician to dust for prints. It was probably an exercise in futility—the creep had kept his paws off the note that came with the canary, and no doubt he'd been careful again. Not five minutes had lapsed since the expert had left and Ashley had arrived. She was seeing the raw results of a sick mind.

Jed sucked on his hand, and he crushed Ashley against his chest with his other hand, his fingers tangling in her hair. "It's all right, Jamie. The jerk must've broken in while we were downstairs. The Trojan army could've marched through with the place being as wide open as it is. He punched through the glass and unlocked your door. Crude—" Jed grimaced "—but effective. This place is isolated enough from the ground floor that no one would've heard a sound, even if all that drilling wasn't going on across the street."

His lips thinned. "I should've checked your place for vulnerability and done something about this glass door. It's my fault."

Ashley shook her head against Jed's chest, but he kept on damning himself. He wondered if he was going to slip up again. His personal feelings had gotten in the way and distracted him, just as Anthony had warned. "Anyway, I've already called the carpenter to replace the glass with something a lot more secure. I'd like to close off the open access to your place and have him install a solid door downstairs, too."

"No. I don't want a dark fortress, I need the sun, the space . . ."

He sighed, knowing why she wanted the sun. "It was just a thought. I'll have to call a locksmith, too."

He moved back to get a good look at her, suddenly struck by something. No tears. Even though most women he'd known would've gone through a box of tissue by now. "Hey, are you okay?"

She nodded, although she felt violated. She stared at the destruction. The apartment decor was eclectic and uniquely her own. After the brownstone's renovation, she'd brought her past out of storage. The angular family room just beyond the foyer was the heart of her home. It was big and airy, all cream and wood and earth tones, enhanced by two quarry-rock fireplaces, a vaulted ceiling, a polished red-oak floor and leaded windows with window seats. Besides the love seats, table and a couple of comfortable-looking chairs, the room was also graced with three grandfather clocks, a player piano, a pine hutch filled with Indian collectibles and other custom-built cabinets for more collectibles.

Ashley blinked. Almost everything had been thrown to the floor. Even the exquisite inlaid silver tortoise was lying on its back. Indian dolls were scattered like so much garbage, and her mother's precious cradleboards were strewn throughout the room like leaves after a storm.

"It's not just the mess," she admitted. "It's not even the fact that someone wants to hurt me and has . . . v-violated me. It's . . ."

"I know, Jamie, I know." Jed made a sweeping gesture with his hand. "All this is your heritage. All you have left of your parents. I remember."

His lips tightened. He remembered everything Ashley had told him that night at Stephano's. When she was fourteen, her parents had been killed in a car crash on their way home from a buying trip for their antique shop. Sean had been staying with her, on winter break from college. Ashley had been told by a gruff policeman who'd knocked on her door late that night. With no other relatives but nineteen-year-old Sean, the Department of Children and Family Services had placed Ashley in with foster parents. The social worker had resorted to using a policewoman to drag Ashley from her home.

And the nightmare had continued. Her foster father had made leering advances, then sexually molested her one terrible night when he'd had too much to drink. The cops hadn't even charged him, only issued a warning. A frantic Sean had then hired an attorney and gone to court. He'd transferred to a college in Chicago and was finally awarded temporary custody. But DCFS had stubbornly retained the right to make random visits to check on Ashley's "status and needs." The officious social worker had constantly told Ashley that they had the power to take her away at any time.

She'd lived in fear. And gained a permanent wariness of the authorities.

It was no wonder she'd refused to surrender her control, determined to hide any vulnerability and reluctant to trust anyone. Jed grimaced. And he hadn't helped five years ago. Leaving her and not getting a chance to explain.

But that didn't mean she didn't need someone now.

Jed moved a gentle hand through her hair. "The jerk had the chance to go crazy, Jamie. The noise of the drilling outside masked everything. I'm sorry."

He was calling her Jamie. The name was a caress when spoken in his husky voice. She remembered when he'd started using it. She squeezed her eyes shut, not wanting to fight the comforting sensation. Let him use it—for now. She nestled against his broad chest, feeling his steady heartbeat under the rough denim coveralls.

"There's more, isn't there?" she asked, surprised at the weak little voice that came out of her mouth. With Jed's arms around her, she felt so warm, so safe. She warned herself that she could be heading for danger by trusting a man like Jed. So why was she still in his arms? She had to resist this disturbing dependency. Later, she decided, snuggling closer.

Jed rested his chin on the top of her head, squeezing her tight, feeling an absurd sense of well-being, an essential rightness in the middle of chaos. For the moment she didn't hate him. And, oh, Lord, he sure didn't hate her.

Jed swallowed and loosened his grip. He stepped back quickly, before she realized how she was affecting him. "No, honey, no more," he croaked. "Just this room. The kitchen's untouched, same with the dining room and your bedroom and the sun room. All your cacti are intact. Hey, I didn't know cacti had flowers. Tell me how you get 'em to bloom like that."

Ashley almost broke into laughter at his patently fake interest in botany. She drew back and straightened up. "Tell me the truth, Cooper, and stop protecting me. What memento did the creep leave me this time?"

"Later, when you're more—"

"Now. Tell me now. I won't break. Believe me."

"Only if you'll sit down and let me make you some herbal tea. Sit." He settled her on the full-size sofa, the only piece of furniture upright besides the piano, and kissed her forehead like a mother. He gave her a warning look. "Stay."

Ashley sighed and leaned her head back, listening to Jed moving around her cramped kitchen. She took the ceramic mug he eventually offered and sipped the hot tea, which was sweetened just to her liking.

"You have a good memory, Cooper."

"How could you forget a girl who dumps two tablespoons of sugar into her tea at breakfast? Or should I say, tea into her sugar?"

She tapped the dish towel he'd wrapped around his hand. "I bit you. I'm sorry."

"It's okay. I'm sure you're sterile." He smiled. "I think you've wanted to do something like that to me for a long time, and now you've got it out of your system. Seriously, Ashley, you were just doing what came naturally. My only other advice is kick. If the jerk ever gets close, kick him right where it hurts."

"Is that what all your training taught you? Can't you teach me a little karate in five easy lessons so I can put my hand through a concrete slab?"

"I'm serious. Stop the jokes." He tossed the towel away and kneeled in front of her, looking into her eyes. "Listen to me very carefully. This creep is for real. I'll admit I didn't think so at first, but I do now. He planned his break-in perfectly. I think he knew the time of your first appointment, which means he knew how much time he had. This is the work of a sick but clever mind who knows you and your routine."

"Thank you for your concern, but don't you think you're being just a little dramatic?"

"You think I'm being dramatic? Okay, humor me and answer some questions while everything's still fresh in your mind. Who was the client you saw?"

"Amanda Bergman."

"Who'd know Amanda was here? Who'd care?"

"I don't know!" She licked her lips. "Well, maybe I do know. Kind of. She broke up with Harold Bates, another client a month ago. Harold had fallen for her like a broken elevator. When I called her last week to set up another appointment, she was watching a video with Harold. Amanda says he's become her best friend."

Ashley placed her hand on Jed's for emphasis. "Harold's a doll. He's one of the nicest guys you'll ever meet. Actually he's far too nice for Amanda. She'd be the type to hold a grudge if I didn't fix her up with the right kind of guy. She's five ten and works out every day, and she has the temperament to kick the furniture around and threaten to—" she faltered "—to k-kill me."

She'd gone white. For all her sass, Ashley was about as tough as a Twinkie. "Honey, I'm sorry," Jed said. "I don't want to scare you. But you see my point. And it *is* interesting that the threats began last week, around the same time you called Amanda. But the thing is, the creep could be *any-one* you know, even Mr. Salerno. I want you to take this very, very seriously."

"Enough warnings, Cooper. Now stop stalling. I want to see the message the creep left."

Jed took a good look at the stubborn set of her chin. Then he sighed. Standing, he tugged a square of paper out of a plastic bag and pinched it carefully by a corner. "Ready?"

At her nod, he said, "This guy's no poet. Here goes:

Ashley the pill
Went up the hill
To fetch a pail of water
She was knocked down
And broke her crown
And tumbled over and over.

"All the letters are cut out from magazines again. Very neatly. The creep must be good with paper dolls." With a sound of disgust, Jed put the paper back into the baggie and stuck it in his pocket. He tucked his hands under his armpits and looked everywhere but at her.

"Ash, maybe we should call the police. I'm out of my league here. Anthony is, too, even though he'd never admit it." *And I'm too involved*, he added to himself. *I can't do my job when just touching you ties me in knots Houdini couldn't unravel.* "This is the work of a psycho," he went on quickly. "You need trained police psychologists to figure out this guy."

He picked up the phone. "While the lab men dusted for prints, I put a tap on your phone line, but I don't think that'll help, either. According to what Sean told Anthony, the creep's taped messages have only lasted a few seconds, not even enough time to pinpoint an area. But the cops have all kinds of tricks these days—portable lasers, computers, microscopic fiber tests. Maybe their people can—"

"No!" Ashley sprang up and grabbed the phone out of Jed's hand, slamming it back down. Jed blinked in surprise. She bit her lip. "Jed, the police aren't about to assign a crack forensic team to my case. They only use that kind of manpower to hunt for mass murderers. And I'm uncomfortable with the police . . . It reminds me of when my parents died."

She clamped her mouth shut, not telling him the other reason she didn't want the police called. If the police took charge, Jed wouldn't need to be there.

She chewed on her lip. She hated to admit it—in fact, it scared her silly—but the truth was she liked having Jed around. He was like potato chips, she thought wryly. One nibble and you craved the whole package. Those few minutes of snuggling into his chest were the most wonderful minutes she'd spent in five years. She wiped a hand over her forehead. What was she thinking?

"Look, I'm not about to put you in more danger because of my incompetence! My little adventures, dangerous though they were, were all cut-and-dried, and I had an experienced P.I. around each time. This is different—an unknown villain in a city of three million people. Anthony's out of town. I don't have the experience or the objectivity and . . . Hell, I'm calling the cops." He reached for the phone.

She tilted her chin stubbornly and spoke very softly. "Are you going to run out on me again, Jed?"

All the color drained from his face, and she gasped at the hurt in his midnight eyes. His lips tightened then, and he flipped an end table upright, as if it weighed nothing. Grabbing the mug out of her hand, he set it on the table before pulling her tightly to him.

Jed stared down at her.

"I *never* ran out on you. This time you're going to listen to me. You can't get away, because I won't let you. You can't scream, because that'll scare the tenants. And this time you don't have a big dog to eat me up."

"I—"

He hauled her down onto the couch next to him. "Shut up and listen. I repeat—I did not run out on you. I know this sounds totally crazy, but I fell for you in one day and one night. Fell hard. Romantics might call it love at first sight. Cynics might label it hormones. I don't know what the hell it was except maybe magic. I've had plenty of women, and nothing like that day and night with you has ever happened to me. How can you say I ran out on you when I came back?"

He paused for a breath, then continued, "I'll say it again. I *am* an attorney. I did do all kinds of indigent advocate work during law school and during the summer right after I graduated. Then the story changes a little. I joined my father's firm, which had been his plan for me since the second I was born, and I quit after two years in the corporate world. What I didn't tell you five years ago is the very long story after that."

Jed took another breath. "After I left the firm, I got sidetracked. But when I was with you I had every intention of dropping the impostor act and following my dreams." He looked at her face, frozen between belief and skepticism.

"My God, Ashley, do you think I made it all up? I'm not that good at improvisation. I exposed myself to you. When I talked to you that night I *became* the crusading attorney. I *believed* in it and in myself, all over again! Jeez, I didn't know my agent was going to call a press conference. I didn't know it would make the papers here and that you'd read about it before I could tell you the truth myself. I

tried to explain all this to you. Instead, I got to face
Rin Tin Tin. I was going to come back to you and
a law practice in Chicago, Ash. But you never gave
me the chance. When I wrote three months later,
after I thought you'd have cooled off, you sent my
letter back, unopened." *And now it's too late*, he
added to himself. *Things have changed*. His hands
fell to his sides.

She swallowed, not ready to believe or forgive.
"The seduction of a short redheaded virgin was not
part of the game plan?"

"No! It just happened. Five minutes after I met
you—no, less than five minutes—and the game
plan, as you call it, disintegrated. Did you see one
word of what you told me about your agency in my
articles?"

He paused while she shook her head slowly,
hopefully. "Right, and you didn't because I wasn't
working when we were together. That was *me* with
you, not a reporter. And our being together, the
magic we made together, meant as much to me as
it did to you. I've carried the memory of that day
and night with me for five years. I went nuts in Anthony's office when you started toying with those
memories. It hurt like hell."

Dazed, Ashley braced herself against the couch.
This was too much to take in. She needed to deal
with the emotional ramifications later, in private.

She swallowed. Now she wanted facts, just plain hard facts. She needed them, so that she could try to understand exactly who and what Jed Cooper was.

Ashley cleared her throat, drawing in a breath to calm herself. "Jed, how did you get sidetracked? I still don't understand. Why did you have to lie to me? Why didn't you just become that crusading lawyer when you left your father's firm?

He sighed, rubbing a hand over his face. "I didn't just say, 'Bye, Pops,' and leave. It wasn't quite that easy."

He bit back an acid laugh. "I'll make this story short and unsweet. After two years in a firm founded by my great-grandfather, a firm with a reputation for using any means to obtain winning ends, I turned my back on the practice. And, to put it simply, Father saw my action as a personal repudiation of everything he stood for. In short—" Jed's mouth lifted at one corner "—he told me I wasn't his son anymore. He called me everything—quitter, ingrate. If I walked away from the family heritage, I was cut out of his will. And then . . ." Jed shook his head. "No. Don't ask me to tell you what he said then."

Abruptly he got up and began to prowl the room. "Hell, let's clean up. You don't need to hear about my dysfunctional relationship with my father. Especially when you have slightly more pressing problems of your own."

She followed him like a shadow. "Oh, no, you don't. This—" Ashley waved a hand at the disorder "—can wait. I think you're slightly more pressing than my furniture." She laughed and pointed to the couch. "Sit and talk. I want the whole damn story."

"No more. It's boring."

She gave him a little push toward the couch. "You're anything but boring." She tapped him on the head with a couch pillow. "Talk or I'll beat it out of you." That earned her a small bitter smile.

He sat, then Ashley sat beside him, and crossed her arms. "I've got all the time in the world, Cooper."

He sighed. "You don't need a rottweiler, Jamieson. You're something of a bulldog yourself."

"Jed..."

He grimaced. "I'll make it short. After my father threw me out, I drifted, eventually hooking up with some musician friends from my undergraduate days—I play a pretty decent sax. One day a casting director spotted me at a Greenwich Village club and told me about a soap opera that needed a scruffy-musician type who'd been around the block. Just for the hell of it, I went to the audition."

Ashley's eyes widened. "The Great Impostor's big start."

Jed nodded, a mocking smile on his lips. "I ended up as black sheep Donovan Spencer III on 'River Run' for one year. After I 'died' from a drug overdose I had a lot to write about—all kinds of backstage stuff. The article got me a contract, and I went on to bigger and better adventures. It became addictive," Jed admitted. "Lots of identities, and not one a screwup or a quitter."

He shrugged. "Anyway, I kind of lost sight of my old dream of righting wrongs. By the time I met you, public-interest work had become a convenient cover. And after you, well—" he chuckled acidly "—hell, it took my agent a month to track me down."

With a shiver, Ashley saw what was behind the self-mocking glint in Jed's eye. She made a fist to keep herself from reaching out to smooth back the lock of hair on his forehead. One touch now and... She smothered the thought.

No touching, not if she wanted to hang on to the slightest remnant of control.

She swallowed. "There's more, Jed. What's changed in the past five years? Something has. You spoke so, I don't know, so passionately about your dream. It had nothing to do with idealism, and it sure had nothing to do with being a quitter! There's more to your story than you're telling me."

Ashley saw him wince, and she knew she was right. Gingerly she laid her small hand on his big one, sparking the electric connection she'd feared....

It stole her breath away.

Caressing his knuckles, Ashley murmured, "Don't lie to me again. Not even by omission. Don't ever lie to me."

He looked at her intently, searching her velvet brown eyes. "Hell, I guess you deserve to know. I've told you this much."

He pulled his free hand through his rumpled hair, while he kept his other hand carefully still under hers. He was grateful for the touch of her soft soothing fingers. He should be comforting her, and instead, she was the one doing the comforting. She definitely didn't hate him anymore. He felt a gleam of hope. She remembered the magic as well as he did.

He continued thoughtfully, "I kept thinking about coming back and setting up a practice, but one assignment after another got in the way. And don't forget, *you* were in Chicago, Jamieson." His lip quirked. "You and that rottweiler. So I ended up not doing anything except sending Christmas cards to my friends, who were doing exactly what I wanted to be doing. One year turned into four. And then there was last year."

His lips thinned. "I've kept in touch with my aunt Vivian all this time, my father's older sister. Eleven months ago he had an operation for lung cancer. He's not doing great—he may have to undergo further treatment." Jed's face was an unreadable mask. "Vivian says he didn't throw my get-well card away. The first time he hasn't tossed out something I sent him." Jed sighed. "After this undercover assignment everything goes into a book, Ashley. My agent swears it's going to be a bestseller. And when Father sees . . ."

Her heart sank. She saw his plan as if he'd mapped it out. "You hope he'll welcome you back as his son then, and ask you to return to the firm."

His eyes met hers, brutally honest. "I know. It sounds stupid. A grown man seeking forgiveness from his father. Especially someone like me, a stone that's rolled through fifty states. Someone who's achieved a little fame and fortune on his own. But now, with the thought of him dying . . . I just keep remembering all those years he was there for me— demanding and stern, yeah, but a good father."

Jed cleared his throat. "And to have him go to his grave thinking what he does, wishing I'd never been born . . ."

"Never been born?" she asked softly. "What do you mean? What else did your father say to you that night, Jed?"

A pulse beat erratically in his cheek. He paused and then said evenly, "He told me my mother's dying in childbirth—when she had me—wasn't worth it. That she died for nothing." He met her eyes briefly and then looked away.

Ashley saw the light go out of those sapphire eyes, and she hated the father who could do this to his son.

"All I know is that my father respects success," he said in a low voice. And if I come back to him as the author of a bestseller, I can talk my way back into the firm. My rustiness'll be offset by an invaluable network of connections all over the country. I'll start from scratch and dedicate my life to the damned firm. I can do that for him as long as he's alive. And maybe what I saw as an idealistic kid fresh out of law school and what I'd see today would be two different things."

"And your dreams, Jed? What about what you want? What about what's inside you and the people who need that kind of dedication?"

His eyes turned hard. "Past tense, Ash. It's history. What you want in this world and what you get are not always compatible. Now let's clean this place up and then figure out a way to catch that stalker. I promise I'll do my best—what I lack in expertise I'll make up with all that dedication you admire so much. If you still don't want me to call the cops, that is. You see, I'm not the man you thought I was. I may be even worse."

Ashley bit her lip and nodded. "Stay," she murmured, squeezing his hand.

THE DOLLS CUT the tension that had spread between them. Her mother's Indian dolls. Jed put the furniture upright and Ashley scooped the dolls up one by one, carefully rearranging them around the room, reminiscing about the history of each figure as she set it in place. Hesitant at first, she opened up with Jed's encouragement. "She found this pair in Arizona on a Hopi reservation. And this one at an estate sale right here in the suburbs."

Jed urged her on while he worked, giving her an encouraging nod or a smile. Really interested, she thought, not humoring her the way Stephen would have.

"I used to love going on trips with them. We'd pack up the van and just go. Usually west. Sometimes they even took Sean and me out of school— said we'd get more of an education with them."

He grunted, heaving a grandfather clock upright, carefully avoiding shards of glass. Amazingly it was still ticking. "I suppose out West is where you discovered a love of cacti. Did you haul a huge saguaro out of the desert in that van of yours?"

She laughed. "No! We would never disturb the grand old guardians of the desert. But, yes, I did discover cacti there. Flowering when most plants would wither up and die. They..." She looked away, suddenly uncomfortable with the way he studied her with those knowing eyes.

Ashley shivered, keeping her eyes averted. "And I'm the one who started my mother on the dolls." She fingered a hank of hair on one doll, brushing off the black fingerprint powder that covered everything. She set the last doll carefully on the shelf, next to one of her mother's miniature clocks.

She was starting to feel so strange, as if she was wandering through a thick fog. Posttraumatic stress disorder, she thought wryly. First the wanton destruction of her home, then Jed's story. It must've taken more of an emotional toll on her than she'd thought.

"It's been fourteen years since they died," she said through the fog. "You know, Jed, sometimes I wonder if we can be too happy. Do you think that's possible? That it's not good to be too happy?" Suddenly she wasn't sure if she was thinking about her family or about five years ago.

If you cared too much, people left you.

Ashley wiped an eye, telling herself she was just a bit overwrought. She hadn't cried for years. She hated blubbering women. She hated three-hand-kerchief movies. She never cried. Not at weddings, not at funerals, not even five years ago.

Jed wiped an elbow across his forehead and then righted the last of the grandfather clocks, glad he had something to do with his hands. Things were starting to get sticky. In fact, he realized things had started turning to molasses the minute he wrapped Ashley in his arms to comfort her. And he didn't need sticky right now. He'd wanted to rekindle the passion, but he'd never meant to reawaken the damn feelings!

He knew any happily-ever-after was lost. He couldn't give reassurances about the future to himself, much less to her. If he had any conscience at all, he would stop things before she got the wrong idea.

"Listen, Ashley, I . . ."

He heard her sniff and turned around, his stomach clenching. Hell.

He was at Ashley's side before the clock let out another tick, wrapping his arms around her. "No, Ash, don't cry," he said fiercely. "It's not bad to be too happy. It's good." He brushed a lone tear from her cheek. "Let me show you how great feeling good can be."

He was only going to comfort her. One fond kiss would do the job.

He placed his mouth over hers. And then he was nibbling her lower lip, stroking it with his tongue, asking permission to enter.

Tremulously her lips parted, and he slipped his tongue inside. She tasted like honey. He felt her taut full breasts push against him as her hands went around his neck. He knew she felt him harden, his treacherous body going way beyond the boundaries of 'fond', but she didn't pull back.

Then Jed did what he'd wanted to do since he saw her in Anthony's office. He placed a row of kisses down her throat to the V of her top. Her petal skin was the satin he'd remembered, sweet and salty and intoxicating. He wanted her, wanted to devour her. Ignoring a little voice that was telling him this was far past the comfort zone, he unbuttoned her tunic's two top buttons, exposing a lacy white bra. She whimpered, and he set his greedy lips to the material, feeling her shiver with each scrape of his tongue.

His hands under her skirt, he pulled down her panty hose, his fingers smoothing the wispy curls inside the silk panties. Ashley moaned, her muscles melting. Frantically she tried to unbutton his coveralls. Her fingers slid inside a gap between the buttons, instead, and brushed over his muscled chest. Her other hand slid lower, far lower, to his erection, hot and hard even through the thick denim.

Jed was torturing her now, his tongue sensuously tracing the edges of her bra. Quicksilver ripples shot through her body. Part of her was screaming caution, but it was drowned out by her uncontrollable need.

Hot damp waves surged through her. Again she fumbled at the buttons on the coveralls, damning herself for making him wear them. Dimly she wondered if they'd even make the bedroom. She needed him inside her. Now.

They sank to their knees, and she was ready to rip the damn coverall apart with both hands.

The phone rang shrilly. They jumped and then broke apart like two guilty teenagers. Gasping, Jed managed to speak, sounding as if he'd been strangled. "Ashley, it could be—" he drew a shuddering breath "—him. Need to find out. The tap . . ."

She nodded and managed to stand, although her knees were shaking. Hauling herself back from the edge with a great effort, Ashley pulled her tunic around her and answered the phone in a breathy voice.

It was the carpenter. He was coming right over. Flushing from her eyebrows to her toes, Ashley disappeared into the bathroom. Jed slouched on the floor where she'd left him, breathing hard, his head thrown back against the couch.

She pulled herself together, splashing cold water on her face and raking her hair behind her ears with her fingers. Breathing shallowly, she stared at her reflection in the mirror. She looked like a gift-wrapped package that had come woefully undone.

When she finally emerged from the bathroom, still shaky, she found Jed sprawled on the couch. Smoky was on his lap, purring like a motorboat.

"You got a kitten," Jed said raggedly, his ruffled hair finger-combed into some order. He gently stroked the cat's soft gray fur. "He came out to say hello. Better than Max the man-eater."

Ashley nodded, suddenly shy and confused. She swallowed and began to babble. "I'm lucky he didn't run out in the middle of the stalker's rampage. He must've been sleeping on top of the hamper—nothing but the sound of the can opener can awaken him then. I'd forgotten all about my Smoky."

She sat down, hijacking the kitten from Jed and cuddling him. "I found him huddling behind the bushes when he was about four weeks old."

She buried her face in Smoky's soft fur, not wanting to talk about what had almost happened between Jed and herself. Now that her senses had returned, she reminded herself that there was no future with this man. He was the opposite of everything she'd ever said she wanted. He was totally unpredictable, totally unreliable. But how could he be so wrong for her when he was so obviously right for her?

She didn't know. She didn't know anything anymore, except that she didn't hate Jed and the carpenter was coming.

Jed tipped up her chin with one finger. "We need to talk about this later. I don't want you to get hurt." He tightened his lips. "I won't lie to you again. Not ever. But I have nothing to offer you right now except the magic. I can give you that. Hell, I want more than anything to give you that. As long as we keep it simple, uncomplicated and honest."

She nodded. Jed was right. In fact, it was very honorable of him to warn her the only thing they could revive was the sexual passion. And she didn't want to be hurt again. She couldn't afford another loss in her life. Ashley swallowed, trying to relieve the dryness in her throat. She'd had enough loss and hurt to last forever.

And that was that. Politely she excused herself and went back into the washroom and threw up.

THE DOORMAN in the high rise across from Ashley's brownstone sprang to attention, holding the heavy glass door open for the attractive blonde.

"Good afternoon, Miss Stabe. Need any help with that shopping bag?"

Miss Stabe gave him a flirtatious smile and licked her red lips. "No thanks, John. But I do appreciate your concern."

She minced into the elevator and pressed the button for the tenth floor.

In the studio apartment, she unloaded her shopping bag on a card table, pushing aside the other paraphernalia—scattered bits of ribbon, magazines, tape, scissors, bulky clothing and notepads.

The blonde spoke into the empty room. "Won't he be pleased to hear how well everything went? It was perfect, absolutely perfect. Miss Jamieson's reaction to my handiwork was everything we could've wanted."

She walked to the window and looked through a mounted telescope pointed directly at Ashley's apartment. "She's still upset. And alone now. That very attractive janitor is gone. Someone is going to be very interested in his arrival." The blonde refocused the telescope, peering through it intently. "He did seem awfully interested in Miss Jamieson's welfare when she found her room . . . rearranged."

Miss Stabe moistened her lips. "Perhaps we'll go directly to Plan B and stop our phone calls. After all, phone calls can be traced."

Turning away from the window, the blonde flexed her shoulders and sat on a chair, fluffing out her curls. She crossed one shapely leg over the other.

She rubbed her thigh sensuously. "He likes your legs, Miss Stabe. He likes everything about you. The perfect partner. An intrepid soul mate in this treacherous world. And I think he'll especially like your new plans."

Then the blonde started humming a show tune. It was "I've Got Rhythm."

5

WHISTLING TUNELESSLY, Jed swished a mop back and forth across Dr. Levy's restroom floor. Then he rubbed the mirror, wiped up the sink and polished the chrome faucets until they shone.

Finally he changed the toilet-paper roll. Any minute now Helen, the orthodontist's office manager, was going to march in and lecture him about how well Darryl had done things. And then, as sure as fire was hot, she was going to make him do something over.

Jed squirted window cleaner over a stubborn blob on the mirror above the sink, sighing and out of whistles. After five days on the job, he was sick of hearing about Darryl. He was tired of being a garbageman and handyman and janitor. And he was definitely sick of having no adrenaline-pumping leads after combing through five years' worth of manila folders. Ashley didn't believe in word processors, and she thought typewriters were cold and mechanical. Her spidery notes on her clients and each of their matches were almost impossible to decipher. Besides, all her clients seemed to be fairly normal Chicagoans.

Jed gritted his teeth as he used his nail to scrape off a remnant of gum stuck to the wall. He was especially tired of being ignored all week by Ashley.

His lip quirked. Last night they'd finally had it out—ending five days of careful avoidance. They'd been in Ashley's apartment, coming up with their ten most promising suspects. Ashley was curled up on the couch, absently biting a nail. A cinnamon curl lay across her cheek, just daring him to try to straighten it out. Jed eyed her surreptitiously for the hundredth time and then shut his eyes, imagining that glorious hair spread out over his pillow.

Warmed by the vision, he'd dumped the handful of files he was scanning to the floor and fell to his knees in front of the couch. "Enough! Ashley, please, let's talk. Stop ignoring me."

She'd squirmed in her seat. "I'm not ignoring you. I work. You work. At night we go through files. I'm sorry if—"

"No, you don't. Talk to me. Remember the concept of honesty, as in 'Jed, don't lie to me'?"

She shoved both hands through her hair. "You have a point," she conceded. "But you said you don't want me to get hurt. And if I let you close enough to work any of your magic on me, I'm going to get hurt."

She looked somewhere over his head, avoiding his eyes. "Besides, I'm sort of involved with someone. The archaeologist I told you about five years ago. And who knows, I just might end up married to him. He's been on a dig for six months, but he should be back any day now."

Jed gritted his teeth. "Listen to me very carefully. Your archaeologist is the last thing you need. A guy who's gone six months out of the year, for crying out loud."

He ignored her attempt to argue. "Oh, stuff the protest and that injured look. I know you put on a good front for everyone else. And it works—for everyone else. But without passion, without *me*, you're almost dead. That damn calendar on the kitchen wall has more lists on it than a professional party planner's. You've got your dentist appointments scheduled for the next three years. There's more to life than regulating it."

"Jed, you've crossed the line!"

He lowered his voice, changing tactics now that a fiery red was mottling her cheeks. "I'll give you lilacs, Jamie."

Desperately wanting it to be true, Jed told himself they could avoid messy emotions and still taste paradise. He leaned forward, nuzzling aside her feathery fall of hair with his nose and whispering in her ear. "Let me show you things no archaeologist would dream of. I'm an expert on the present, not the past."

He hauled her to her feet, suddenly presented with a meek and pliable Ashley. He backed her against a wall, allowing her no escape. She was breathing hard, her breasts heaving under an apricot sweater. A sleepy look blurred her eyes. Very slowly he kissed her spiky-lashed eyes closed and then captured her mouth.

Ashley moaned. Finally she straightened and started to speak, eyes still closed. "Okay, Jed. I'll give us a chance. Get a job here and become that crusading lawyer you invented five years ago."

He dropped his hands, and her eyes snapped open. "You don't know what you're asking," he insisted evenly. "You know I have to go to New York."

"Until you can prove I mean more to you than a good time, I'm not interested. All you want me for is a sleazy cheap affair!"

His eyes were knowing. "It won't be cheap and it won't be sleazy, honey," he drawled. "And you damn well know it."

"Obnoxious man!" Ashley moved away and began collecting the folders he'd thrown to the floor. She added them to the stack she'd set aside before his interruption, then went into the kitchen and came back with a glass of water. After she'd taken a few sips she faced him unblinkingly.

Jed stared while she transformed herself into the cool and controlled Ashley Jamieson. Even in her jeans and sweater, she looked all business. She even looked taller. His jaw hanging open, Jed tried to concentrate on what she was saying to him.

"We have far more important things to discuss, Mr. Cooper. You do remember why you're here? To that end, here's my ten most promising suspects." She slapped the folders against his stomach, forcing him to take them with a grunt.

Arms crossed, Ashley paced the floor, speaking in a measured tone. "I'd say to keep an eye on Matt Bartlett. He's a Vietnam vet whose wife left him when he was MIA. I fixed him up with two women, but they said he was too intense, too scary. I know what they meant—something about the eyes. When I told him I didn't have anyone else he called me a bitch and stalked out."

Jed nodded, mesmerized. She was an incredible piece of work. A challenge. He smiled. He loved a challenge.

"I'll pay Mr. Bartlett a call," he said agreeaband runly.

Ashley glanced at her watch. "Jed, I have to go. According to my calendar, a classic movie I want to see is about to start at the neighborhood repertory cinema. It's about an obnoxious male, actually, so you might be familiar with it. *It Happened One Night.*"

Jed gave her a mocking grin. "I do believe the obnoxious male eventually gets the girl in that one. She can't resist his charms—isn't that the way it goes? You, of all people, know what can happen in one night."

As if she hadn't heard him, Ashley casually took another sip of water. Then she looked at her watch, tipping the contents of her glass on him.

"Oops." She stepped back. "I do believe you're all wet."

He stared at her, speechless.

"Oh, dear," she said. "Compulsive silly me, but I do like to be on time. You know I always did think the ending was stupid and contrived. Claudette Colbert would've been better off without Clark Gable. Things are always much clearer in the morning, after the creatures of the night have crawled back into their holes." Then she'd showed Jed the door.

He'd winked. "Round one to you."

Leaning on his mop now, Jed snapped out of his reverie with a start, telling himself he had to escape Dr. Levy's office before Helen nailed him.

But he was too late, almost running the cart into her formidable body. With gleeful determination,

Helen imprisoned his wrist and led him back to the bathroom.

FROM HER OFFICE an hour or so later, Ashley watched Jed leave. He'd said he was on his way to question some suspects. And then he'd suggested lunch. An amused smile had played on his lips when he'd spoken. As if *she* was dessert.

Ashley set her mug on the coffee table. Leaning back in her rocker, she rolled her shoulders, unable to relax. She'd walked for an hour that morning after a sleepless night, dully admiring the crayon-colored autumn leaves of the oaks, elms and maples. But she was still tense. Jed was definitely bad for her health.

Grimacing at the tightness in the back of her neck, she tapped Stephen's letter, which was nestled in her suit pocket. She'd taken to carrying it around and reading it at odd moments ever since it had arrived three days ago. Stephen had written a very unStephen-like letter—assertive, almost possessive. Would she marry him or not?

She thought that maybe she would.

If wild crazy love and passion weren't there, well, they weren't everything. She reddened, thinking how she and Stephen had never even made love. They'd come close during the early years of their relationship. But somehow it hadn't seemed right.

Then he'd wanted marriage and she hadn't, and they'd broken up. Eventually Stephen had sworn he wouldn't rush her anymore, and they'd gotten back together, but things had never been the same. Because by that time Jed had come and gone. Her relationship with Stephen had become more convenient than anything else. Still, Stephen had persisted, insisting he'd hang around until she fell in love with him.

Ashley traced the edges of Stephen's letter as if it were a talisman. She told herself she'd been right to refuse Jed last night. An affair, no matter how blazing hot, just wasn't her style.

She bit a nail. Or was it?

When the phone rang, she pounced on it, happy for the distraction.

It was Amanda Bergman, checking in as she always did after a new date. She wanted Ashley to be the first person—after Harold—to know that Brent Kelly was the man she was going to marry. In fact, Amanda coyly promised she'd invite Ashley and Harold to the wedding.

Ashley hung up, a sad smile on her lips. Poor Harold. She wondered how he'd handled the news.

Four clients, three aspirin and a pounding headache later, Ashley finally trotted upstairs for lunch. Tuna salad on a bagel. Her usual. She didn't think twice about the package sitting outside her door until she realized it was ticking.

JED RACED DOWN the left lane of the Outer Drive in his rented Grand Prix, praying one of Chicago's finest didn't appear. His heart hammering a wild tattoo, he swerved in and out of lanes, passing cars as if he was doing the Indy 500. A blare of horns echoed behind him as he turned onto Fullerton. "Don't touch it," he'd told Ashley from the car phone. "Get everyone the hell out of the building, tell them you smelled gas. I was on my way home, anyway, and I'll get there faster than any cop."

Minutes later, he squealed to a stop in front of the brownstone. Brushing past Ashley, he took the stairs three at a time. In an instant, he knew it wasn't a bomb. This was a very different kind of sound. He knelt down, head cocked. Loud, stiff ticks. Going in unison. "Metronomes," he gasped. "The creep sent her metronomes."

In the apartment, Jed ripped open the taped box with a knife. Five metronomes, all ticking at 120 beats a minute. A nice marching tempo. He swept the box to the floor, just as he caught movement out of the corner of his eye.

Whirling around, he stopped as recognition dawned. "Jeez. You almost gave me a heart attack, Ashley."

She stood soldier straight, her face as white as a lily. Not bothering to ask for permission, Jed took her in his arms. After long moments, he felt her relax. He sucked in a breath, consumed by the urge to hold her that way for a couple of years.

He swallowed. *No messy emotions, Cooper, remember?*

Ashley pulled away first. "I'm okay. Really I am." She folded her arms in front of her. "Read me the note I saw you pocket. Let's see what Shakespeare has to say today."

Sheepishly he tugged the square of paper out of his pocket. He cleared his throat and read:

March to the right
March to the left
March off a cliff
And fall to your death

He slammed his fist on the kitchen counter, cursing creatively. "Ashley, I checked out five of our suspects this morning. We can cross 'em off. Two are married now, and they both agreed to take lie-detector tests. The third is happily living with a lingerie model. The fourth has been in Oregon for a year, and the fifth is deceased.

Jed glanced at Ashley and became alarmed by her Casper-the-ghost complexion. Taking her hand, he led her to the family room and pulled her down onto the love seat next to him.

"Ashley," he said in a gentle, calming voice. "I have to tell you that I'm positive your stalker is all talk, no action. This is kindergarten stuff. It makes me mad as hell that he's harassing you, of course, but in my professional opinion—and it is worth something—he's just a nuisance."

Jed was lying. He wasn't really sure of anything.

He thought fast, intent on bringing back the life to Ashley's eyes. "Listen, I want you to forget about him for today. Cancel your appointments and get out of that business suit. Put on some sweats and meet me downstairs in fifteen minutes."

"No. I—"

He put a finger on her lips. "No ifs, ands or buts. Downstairs in fifteen minutes or I'm coming in after you."

He marched her into her bedroom and tugged a sweat suit off a hanger, tossing it onto her bed. "Put that on your body."

"Jed—"

"Or I'll put it on for you."

"Okay, okay! But I don't like being ordered around."

Ashley practically shut the apartment door in his face. For a moment Jed stood there, admiring the new carved-oak inset that had replaced the beveled glass. Then, reminding himself to call a locksmith, he went downstairs to wait for Ashley.

An hour later, Ashley found herself at Chicago's Art Institute. Jed was leaning against one of the majestic stone lions guarding the entrance on Michigan Avenue. As Ashley watched, the sunlight brought out the sapphire in his eyes—eyes that he hadn't taken off her since they'd left the brownstone. Honestly, he was as protective as a mother bear with a cub.

"Hey, wake up, Jamieson. First stop on our journey." Jed gestured with one hand. "Chicago's world-renowned museum of art."

"You're nuts."

He nodded agreeably. "My middle name. Come on."

He took her hand and led her into one of her favorite places. How had he known? She decided he must've seen a notation about visiting the museum on the calendar he hated so much. She circled dates she was going to the museum in red magic marker to differentiate them from the notes telling her to call Sean—green marker—and to reserve seating for the Lakeside Community Theater series—blue marker. Of course, she had a slew of other colors for other notes. She bit her lip. Maybe she *was* a tad obsessive.

Ashley took a series of fast steps to keep up with Jed's long easy stride, the parquet floor creaking under their sneakers. They toured the museum, seeing all her favorite exhibits, lingering longest in the Impressionist gallery. "My favorite," she whispered to Jed, gazing at a Monet.

He turned away from the frosty seascape and stared at her profile. "Yup, beautiful." He checked his watch. "Hey, princess, time to go. Your carriage awaits."

In the car, it took Ashley all of two seconds to notice they were heading south, not north, along Lake Shore Drive. Lake Michigan shimmered on their left, and a dark forest of skyscrapers towered on their right. "This isn't the way home, Jed."

"Who said anything about going home? It's not time for home. It's time for dinosaurs." He pulled into the parking lot of the Field Museum of Natural History.

Stopping in the lobby, Ashley moved in a small circle, taking in the sounds of babbling tourists, the shrieking of children on field trips. "I haven't been here for years!" she exclaimed.

She stood on tiptoe, pointing. "Look, Tyrannosaurus rex! I bet you didn't know I wanted to be a paleontologist when I was ten. Did you know one of the earliest dinosaurs was Euraptor? And that they're 350 known species and their descendants are birds?"

She laughed and sprinted off. He had to jog to catch up to her.

"Did I ever tell you I used to take classes at the Art Institute, and we'd come here to sketch the animals? I liked working in chalks, and I'd do the antelopes . . ."

Jed bought them hot dogs in the museum cafeteria when they finished viewing the exhibits. He fingered a drop of mustard off Ashley's upper lip. "I can't take you anywhere, can I?"

She grinned. "You can take me anywhere, Jed. Thank you. And I mean that."

He sprang up. "Okay, one more stop."

"You really *are* nuts!" She put a finger to her temple. "Oh, wait, I get it. You worked undercover as a tour guide."

"Shut up, Jamieson."

Back in the car and heading south again, Jed made her close her eyes. "No peeking. Not until I tell you. Promise?"

"Promise. But really. We have to get—"

His knuckles scraped a caress across her cheek. "No. We don't *have* to do anything this afternoon, Jamieson. This is all for you. Forget the have-to's and the I-shoulds. Promise?"

She nodded, eyes tightly shut. "Yeah."

Five minutes later he said, "Open."

They were in front of the sprawling Grecian-styled Museum of Science and Industry. She gasped. "You're psychic, Jed. I wanted to live here once upon a time. I threw a tantrum when Mom said I couldn't. Let's do the coal mine first, then the German submarine, then the whispering gallery, then the heart, then the old-time theater, and we'll finish up at the chicken incubator."

Jed slumped in his seat, raised his eyes and breathed a prayer of thanks to the museum gods. Finally he'd done it. Finally she'd forgotten about her lists and appointments and responsibilities. He grinned at her enthusiasm and trailed gamely after her through every exhibit.

Patiently he waited while she spent a solid hour at the giant glass incubator, leaning against the railing and watching scrawny chicks turn a little crack into an escape hatch.

"Isn't it neat!" she said when the tenth damp chicken dried off and turned into what Jed thought a chicken was supposed to look like.

By the time they got home, the sun was sinking behind a horizon of rooftops. Ashley and Jed watched from the brownstone's archway.

"The real world's still here, isn't it?" she murmured. Then she unlocked the door and slowly walked through the lobby. Jed followed like a protective shadow. She looked so small, so vulnerable.

"Listen, Ashley," Jed said suddenly, "you're wrong. The real world isn't here, not until we let it back in. Tonight, I want you to dress in something beautiful, and I'll make you dinner. I make a mean lasagna. Garlic bread, salad, wine—the works. You need this."

She crossed her arms and gave him the hint of a cocky smile. "Who made you doctor? Or have you been one of those, too?"

"Cute, very cute. I'll pick up a few things at the store and be right back."

She swallowed and looked away, anywhere but at Jed. Did he expect some sort of...reward for this afternoon? For being more wonderful to her than any knight? There was still a rational part of her brain that told her letting Jed loose in her house and in her life was insanity of the first degree. *Say no,* said her sane voice. *Say no and thank you very much but I'm tired and good night.*

Jed narrowed his eyes as Ashley withdrew from him. "Hey, come on. Do it for me. I promise, the only thing I'll press on you will be lasagna. Scout's honor."

Somehow her no came out as yes.

Jed ran to the supermarket and returned in minutes. He then proceeded to dice onions, mince garlic, prepare the meat sauce and cook the noodles.

Soon his mouth was watering, but it wasn't from thoughts of lasagna. It was because Ashley's gorgeous body was soaking so near and yet so far in a rose-scented bubble bath. He'd bought the pink frothy concoction at the market and had personally poured it into the tub. And now those bubbles were nuzzling her naked ivory flesh all over. He pressed himself against the kitchen counter, trying to control his wayward body.

"Dammit, you promised her," Jed muttered to Smoky, scratching the cat under his thin red collar.

The scent of rose petals drifted into the room.

"Are you in the habit of talking to yourself? Or has Smoky turned into a parrot?"

Jed looked up and his mouth dropped open. Ashley wore a silky green outfit that flowed over her curves like water over a fall. A low frothy neck hinted at her full breasts, and wide harem pants slithered with her every movement. The iridescent green picked up sparkles in her brown eyes and set off the fire in her glorious hair. Jed rolled up his shirtsleeves for want of something better to do—such as crush her in his arms and break his promise.

"You're uh, you're gorgeous. Here." He poured them each a generous glass of chardonnay, dribbling a little on the counter in his haste. "Have something to drink while I make the salad." He downed his drink without pausing for breath and poured another.

"I'll set the table," Ashley said, bending over and snatching a set of pewter candlesticks from under the oak buffet, pretending not to notice the evidence of Jed's arousal. She knew she was playing with fire.

But maybe she didn't care.

They talked easily through dinner, relaxed by the wine and the thought of the evening stretching endlessly ahead of them.

Jed watched the candlelight shimmer in Ashley's hair, and he knew himself to be a fool. How could he have ever thought he could walk away from her?

Thoughtfully he chewed on a piece of garlic bread, a brilliant idea slowly forming. Ashley could come to New York with him! Maybe they could even—he choked on the bread—get married one day. Have kids. He grabbed a full glass of water and gulped it down.

Jed stopped coughing, and the image of four little girls popped into his head, each one with Ashley's crinkled mass of russet hair. He pictured visiting Chicago and taking them to Wrigley Field, explaining the double play, the hit and run, the suicide squeeze.

His eyes narrowed.

He was thinking sticky feelings.

He was thinking commitment.

Now he just had to tell Ashley she was moving.

Jed dumped two tablespoons of sugar into her coffee, then he set the cup in front of her. "Here. Drink."

She flushed, feeling very warm, very good, with Jed hovering over her like a big guardian angel, smelling of lime after-shave and coffee. *Why fight him? Why shouldn't I take what he's offering? Who am I to stand between a son and his father?*

She decided she'd been selfish. Besides which, she was everything Jed had said she was—compulsive and repressed. Maybe it was time to live.

She put her mug down and twisted around, looking up into Jed's eyes. She sent him an unmistakable invitation.

"Ashley, I, um, really think we need to—"

Whip quick, she stood, putting her finger across his mouth. "No talking, Cooper. Just give me the magic. Give it to me. No commitment. No security. No tomorrow."

He jerked back as if she'd punched him. "Cripes, no! I mean, first I have something to—"

"Anyone ever tell you that you talk way too much?" Standing on tiptoe, her lips closed over his like petals. She quickly unbuttoned his shirt, smoothing her hand over his hard chest. She dropped her head and licked his flat nipples, suckling lightly while he groaned.

"Jeez, you . . ." His arms went around her automatically, and then he jerked them back, groaning again at the feel of her body pressed against his. She playfully bit him as her hands fumbled with his belt.

"Ash . . . first, I have something to . . . before we . . . I have to tell you before . . ."

She slipped her hand inside his briefs, and he was lost.

He wrapped his arms around her, wondering where he should put his mouth first.

He didn't even hear the key in her lock or the door open.

A tall figure entered the apartment, allowing Smoky to run out, and two minutes later all hell broke loose.

6

ASHLEY AND JED FROZE as a floorboard creaked.

"Ashley?" the stranger whispered.

Jed cursed under his breath. Twisting away from the open door, he instinctively kept Ashley tucked against his body. He snapped off the dining room light and dropped to the floor, sheltering her underneath him. The dining room was to the left of the foyer. Peering around the table, Jed had a view of the front door, lit only by the moonlight coming in through the windows.

"Stay down," he hissed at Ashley, silently damning his own carelessness. He should've called the locksmith.

"Jed, I think it's—"

"Shh."

He crept toward the intruder, carefully keeping to the room's shadows. In less time than it took to draw a breath, Ashley couldn't distinguish him at all. Before someone got hurt she called out, "Jed, I'm sure it's—"

The stranger flicked on the hall light, illuminating Jed midspring. Both men crashed to the floor,

Jed's hands locked around the intruder's throat. "Ashley, you know this guy?"

She scrambled to her feet, heart pounding, face flaming. Stephen had had a key to her place for years, but he'd never used it without first telling her he was going to let himself in.

"It's Stephen, Jed, my, uh, b-boyfriend . . ."

Jed rocked back on his heels, giving her an incredulous look. Slowly he stood, holding out an arm to Stephen. The archaeologist flinched and then grabbed Jed's hand, lurching to his feet. He massaged his throat with his other hand.

Stephen's voice came out in a rough whisper. "I came straight from the airport, Ashley. Here." He bent over and retrieved a huge bouquet of roses in green tissue paper, holding them out to her. "I didn't know you'd hired a bodyguard." He took off his jacket and tried to neaten his shirt.

Jed surreptitiously buckled his belt while the other man pulled himself together. He shook his head warningly at Ashley and spoke before she could say a word. "Sorry, man. The habit of too many bar fights. Hate like hell to have someone sneak up on me. Jed's the name, Jed Wyatt, the new janitor." He stuck out a hand.

Stephen gingerly shook his hand. "Dr. Stephen Mather. What the heck are you doing here?"

Ashley stood as frozen as a popsicle, watching Jed change into someone she'd never seen.

Jed slapped a vacant smile on his face. "Miz Ashley was just cookin' me a fine meal. Guess she felt sorry for me all alone in Chicago. I come from down South."

"No doubt from the bar belt of Appalachia," Stephen muttered.

Ashley's mouth dropped open. She'd never heard Stephen make a joke before.

Jed brightened as the professor took the bait, overlooking his well-tailored linen shirt and thin gold watch. "Yeah, the mountains of Appalachia," he drawled. "How'd ya know? Lawd, I miss 'em. Country here's as flat as a barn door."

Shoving his hands in his pockets, Jed hoped he'd bought himself some time to check Stephen out. Tomorrow he'd make damn sure the guy had been in the Jordan Valley and not in Chicago. It was possible the stalker was really a boyfriend who wanted to scare his girl right into his arms.

He eyed his competition. Stephen was a good sturdy six feet, with golden hair and hazel eyes. Thirsty eyes, Jed mused, that were taking Ashley in like a desert traveler who'd just spied an oasis.

And he was wasting no time getting to it. "Ashley, dear!" he exclaimed as he enveloped her in a bear hug.

Her cheek squashed against Stephen's chest, Ashley ignored Jed's glare.

"It's just like you, darling, to feed this lonely man, but really, I'm sure he has to be going now." Stephen turned around, his arm across Ashley's shoulder.

Jed refused to take the hint. Instead, he lounged against the wall, hands tucked under his armpits.

"Uh, doesn't he have to be going, Ashley? Perhaps to collect the trash for an early-morning pickup?"

Jed whistled tunelessly.

"Mr. Wyatt? I said—"

"Oh, you talkin' to me?" Jed gave him a friendly grin. "You can just call me Jed, you know. And you must be Miz Ashley's archaeologist. She told me about ya—travelin' halfway around the world diggin' up old pots. You really oughtta let sleepin' pots lie and have more fun, perfessor. Women like that, you know." He winked. "Fun, I mean."

Stephen blushed. "I'm sure you could write a dissertation on fun. And women."

Jed risked a look at Ashley. He swallowed. If looks could kill, he'd be pushing up all the daisies in Appalachia. "Uh, I think I'll be gettin' on about now, Miz Ashley."

Jed pushed away from the wall, patting his stomach. "Thanks for the home-cooked meal. Eyetalian food," he explained to Stephen with a straight face. "Boy, you Chicago folks are sure ethnic." He inched his way to the door. "Nice to meetcha, perfessor," he drawled. "By the way, what's a dissertation?"

Before the door shut behind him, he heard Stephen mutter, "Did you buy him clothes, too, Ashley? Really, dear . . ."

Ashley nervously arranged the roses in a cutglass vase while Stephen sat patiently on a chair calmly sipping some wine. With a sigh of frustration, Ashley jerked all the roses out of the vase, their dripping stems drizzling on the floor, and began to rearrange the flowers over again.

Desperately she tried to analyze her thoughts, trying to force her brain to function the way it did before Jed had invaded her life.

The last time she'd thought about Stephen she'd decided she should marry him, right? Isn't that what she'd told herself just that morning? A morning that seemed like a hundred years ago. She glanced at Stephen, who was staring back at her, his handsome face looking rather lovesick. An image flashed in her head of an adoring cocker spaniel she'd once owned who'd looked at her like that. She dropped her gaze, guilt-ridden. There was something else in his expression, too. He seemed more assertive, more . . . aggressive. Half spaniel, half Doberman.

Desperate to cut the thick silence, she squeaked, "Did you have a good dig, Stephen? Make any more amazing finds for the institute?"

"Ashley, stop fussing. The roses look magnificent. You look magnificent. And I apologize if I was a bit presumptuous before. I know how you value your independence. And you have the right to see any man you want to—even an, uh, illiterate janitor." He paused. "Don't look so stricken, dear. I know he's just one of your charity cases."

Stephen stood and enfolded her in his arms, and then he stepped back, swinging her hands loosely in front of him. "Did you get my last letter? Did Sean speak to you for me?"

She nodded mutely.

"Ashley, dear, I . . . I was wondering if I might stay the night. I have a surprise that might change your mind about . . . us."

She wanted to sink into the floor. An earthquake would be handy right around now. And then she realized Stephen's hands were sweaty. She chewed her bottom lip. Stephen always had very sweaty hands when he was tense. Just what was his surprise?

Too soon, her question was answered. "I wanted to give you this, Ashley." Stephen fumbled with a small jewelry box, opening it with one hand. A huge round-cut diamond ring was nestled in a bed of blue velvet. It was as big as a grape.

"Ashley, don't say anything. Just think about it. But I'm asking you to think about it more than you've ever thought about anything in your life." He opened her hand and dropped the ring inside, rolling her fingers up into a fist.

He angled his head down and brushed her lips in a moist kiss.

"Marry me, Ashley. I've got tenure now, and I've established a reputation. It's the right time for us."

"Stephen, maybe—"

"Ashley, I love you. I know I've stubbornly insinuated myself into your life, even when you didn't always want me there. But surely you can see we have ties that can't be broken." He threw back his shoulders. "I insist you come to a decision, Ashley. Enough is enough." He spoke as if he'd rehearsed the words in front of a mirror.

"Stephen, I, uh . . ."

He tipped up her chin. "I don't want to pressure you. Lord knows, as an archaeologist I'm used to patiently waiting for treasures, and seven years is nothing in the grand scheme of things. But, well . . ." Stephen coughed. He studied the ceiling. He studied the floor. He hung his head. "I've met someone who's taught me a lot, Ashley. And if it makes you jealous . . . well, good. Her name is Joan Connelly, from the Harvard team. We've coauthored a paper for the Brussels conference." Stephen still couldn't meet her eyes. "Actually, um, we're writing a grant proposal together, too. We've grown . . . close."

Stephen squeezed her hands. "Ashley, dear, say something. I thought Sean would've prepared the way."

"Stephen, I don't know what to . . . About tonight, I . . ." She shook her head, panic-stricken. She felt as if she was disassociating, one body containing many Ashleys, none communicating with the other. Just exactly what had this Joan taught Stephen?

Stephen cocked his head, inspecting her closely. Then he coughed again. He stepped back, brushing a hand through his hair. "Ashley, darling, I'll be back tomorrow. I can tell by the look in your eyes this has all been too overwhelming." He smiled slyly, shaking a finger at her. "You can't keep any secrets from me. I understand everything."

Her eyes widened. "You do?"

"Of course. My surprise, uh, visit, the ring, mentioning Joan—a bit crass perhaps, and I'm sorry for that—so your bewilderment is natural. You're thinking that this may be the most important decision of your life, and I'll leave you alone to ponder it." Stephen tapped her fist. "You won't really be alone, however. Not with my ring here as a symbol of my feelings. And, Ashley, I, uh, know how to treat a woman now."

She looked up and nodded through blurred eyes. Now she knew what course Joan taught. The same one Jed did. God, she definitely needed time to think!

"Thank you for understanding, Stephen." She touched his cheek. "I understand, too." A Niagara Falls of guilt flooded her. What if Stephen knew she'd almost seduced Jed? Would he be as understanding as she was? And why *wasn't* she jealous of this Joan?

Stephen pecked her on the cheek. "Watch that Jed Wyatt character, darling. There's something about him . . . That man may not be what he seems." He nodded toward the ring in her fist. "But that *is* what it seems."

Smiling tremulously, she nodded as Stephen let himself out. *Not what he seems,* she thought dully.

How ironic that Stephen should see it in Jed and not in her. Didn't she owe him something for his years of patience? Ashley bit her lip. She couldn't blame him for Joan.

She cleared the table, surprised Smoky wasn't there to steal a piece of lettuce to bat around the floor.

Then she washed the dishes, cleaning each glass, each piece of silverware, each plate, very methodically. She was glad she had something to do; it kept her from wondering what Jed was doing.

JED'S BEACH BOY tapes were blaring, and he paced the floor of the tiny apartment, as irritable as a bear flushed out of hibernation. He told himself he'd kill for a good workout, preferably with a punching bag painted with Stephen's face. Just the thought of Ashley cuddled next to him, listening to whatever sweet nothings a six-foot blond archaeologist conjured up, made his gut twist.

At last Jed threw on a denim jacket, turned off "Surfer Girl" and rushed out of the brownstone. Jogging east, he wound his way through obsidian black streets glittering with a light sheen of rain. He found the beach and ran for what seemed like miles, his feet sinking into the damp sand, his breaths coming faster and faster in the cool night air. With surprise, he realized he was jealous. He'd never had reason to be jealous in his life. The women had always come so easily, and he'd cared so little.

Back home, he collapsed on the cot. "He's had his chance," Jed muttered, talking to four walls. "I'll bet ten lasagna noodles he doesn't know her the way I do. There's nothing between them but routine and convenience. And maybe a touch of obsession on the part of Dr. Stephen Mather. The kind that gets you through seven years."

Clenching his jaw, Jed reminded himself that early tomorrow morning he had an appointment that was going to help him catch a stalker. He'd need a clear head.

After an hour of staring at the ceiling, he finally closed his eyes and fell asleep. He didn't even realize all his clothes were still on.

IT WAS SIX-THIRTY in the morning, but Miss Stabe was already neatly made up. Red lipstick had been carefully applied, a smooth coating of powder lay over her large pores, and mascara coated her lashes. Her blond wig was on snug and centered.

"A puppy," she was saying as she swept into the apartment. "One of those cuddly Benji types." She snapped her fingers, nails perfectly painted with red polish. "Just a quick look, Miss Stabe, a quick early-morning look. Really, one day you must begin sleeping here to take advantage of the nightscape. It's so nice to have a city view. Much more interesting than the lake view."

Miss Stabe peered through the telescope, refocused and stared again. "Oh, my. I don't believe it." She put her hand on her heart. "Really, Miss Stabe, this is providence. He said the end was nearing, but I never expected . . . He'll be so pleased with me."

The blonde fixed the telescope on the brownstone's lobby windows, then the upstairs, then the front of the building. "With one exception, not a creature is stirring, not even a mouse." Miss Stabe clapped her hand over her mouth and giggled hysterically.

"I do believe you wet your pants. When the job is done, I do believe you'll need to run home and change them."

Miss Stabe rummaged through the kitchen's almost bare cabinets, grabbing a can. "Yes, yes, salmon. Now calm yourself, calm yourself. Just think of how proud he'll be of your ingenuity."

Miss Stabe was humming another show tune as she let herself out the door. It was "Memory," from *Cats*.

JED SETTLED HIMSELF in the leather wing chair. He faced the clinical psychologist sitting behind a black lacquered desk. The wall clock read 9 a.m.

The attractive doctor took a sip of coffee. "Sure you won't have a cup?"

Jed shook his head, rubbing a hand over his chin and fighting the effects of a night of troubled sleep. He'd been plagued with a series of nightmares—a handsome blond archaeologist unearthing glittering jewels that turned into Ashley's face and curvy vases that were transformed into her body. And

Stephen had selfishly kept all his Ashleys for his own private collection, refusing to share. No wonder Jed had awoken exhausted and crabby.

"So, Dr. Cartwright, you say—"

"Amy, Mr. Wyatt, remember? *Miss* Amy Cartwright." She smiled pointedly, mauve-colored lips framing her even white teeth.

Jed sighed. What had happened to him? There was no answering rise of interest. Nothing. The one woman who had the power to evoke that kind of response might well be eating breakfast in bed with her archaeologist this very minute.

Jed crossed one knee over the other and ran a hand across his brow, drawing on every ounce of concentration he possessed. "Okay, Amy. So, based on the facts I've just given you, you think I should look for a normal person? I don't get it. Only a psycho would do the things I've been telling you about."

Amy Cartwright leaned forward, obviously eager to get her point across. "Exactly, Jed. But this psycho, as you call him, most likely hides it very well. Using one extreme example of a stalker, psychological profiles by FBI experts at Quantico have shown that serial killers often have a chameleon-like ability to adapt to any kind of social situation."

"Tell me more."

"As best as I can explain it, there's a certain progression the sort of pathological personality you've described follows. He grows up with a sense of alienation. He's often abused. He smothers his feelings with an outward show of normalcy until one day something happens to tip him over the edge. And hostility may not even be the motivation. Celebrity stalkers actually want to bond with their victims. Or the victim may be chosen at random, to satisfy a sadistic craving. But I don't think that's the case here. From what you've told me, I think your man has a grudge against your client specifically."

"And you don't think the Vietnam vet is our guy? I shouldn't even bother paying him a visit?"

The psychologist nodded emphatically. "Correct. I'd bet your man, and it very definitely sounds like a man, is someone who seems quite ordinary. He's probably an obsessive-compulsive with a tremendous amount of repressed hostility. The dead bird is a very bad sign. Studies have shown that when the first victim gets hurt, even if it's an animal, the pathological personality's stress is relieved—temporarily. He feels powerful, in control. In fact, your creep may have received a tremendous surge of energy from the act."

Jed's jaw tightened at the thought of a guy getting a high by scaring the hell out of Jamie.

Dr. Cartwright held up two fingers. "Two more things. Number one—how nice the victim is doesn't matter to the criminal. He objectifies his victims. Number two—watch for an escalation in violence, maybe another animal death. That's a definite sign your man has crossed the line and metamorphosed into someone who poses a danger to others. These people have bizarre appetites that inevitably grow—until they're caught."

When his appointment was over, Dr. Cartwright flipped him her card with a coy smile. "Call me anytime for more . . . information."

ASHLEY RECROSSED HER LEGS yet again, wishing that eleven o'clock would never come, then wishing it would be over in an instant. She'd asked Stephen to meet her in her office after her third morning appointment, because she'd made a decision of sorts. She'd changed clothes three times. The pink sweater set made her look too fluffy. The black linen suit was too severe. She'd finally settled on a light wool kelly green suit with a black silk shell.

She looked up as a shadow fell across the floor.

Stephen loomed in the doorway right on time. Tall blond Stephen, in cords and a turtleneck and a tweed blazer with leather patches on the elbows. He might as well have worn a sign that said Safe, Secure, Responsible.

Ashley offered Stephen coffee, jelly beans and a seat. And then she told him everything—about the stalker and about the real reason Jed was there. When she finished, she sat back and let the words soak in.

"Ashley, you should've said something! Why did Jed carry out that silly charade and not tell me he's a private investigator in the first place?"

She shrugged. "I've learned not to question why Jed does anything. But I had to tell you, Stephen, because this affects you and me. I haven't been myself, and I can't make a decision about us now."

He leaned forward, his hazel eyes darkening. "Of course not! Don't worry about that. The important thing is your safety. Is there anything I can do? Why in the world don't you call the police?"

She shook her head. "No police. I'd rather not get them involved. Just . . . No."

Stephen's expression was so earnest it was painful to watch. She told herself he'd be a conscientious husband, a superb father. He'd give her enough security and serenity to choke her. And Stephen never minded the lists on her calendar, either. In fact, for her birthday, he'd bought her a leather-bound five-year appointment calendar.

Ashley sucked on two red jelly beans. "Jed's working on this, Stephen. I know he'll solve it. He says he doesn't even think the stalker is dangerous, although I don't know if he really believes that. Just give me a week, okay?"

She tugged the ring from her suit pocket and pushed it across the coffee table. "Keep this for now, Ste—"

"Jamieson!"

The door crashed open, and Jed strode in, arms loaded with files. He filled the office with his presence, like a panther in a cat show. "Hey, sweets, we gotta start all over."

Jed did a double take when he saw Stephen sitting on the love seat. His gaze moved back and forth between the archaeologist and Ashley until it finally rested on the sparkly ring on the table.

Ashley read Jed's glance and leapt up, her face flaming, her heart pounding.

"No! It's not what . . ." She swallowed. Actually, it *was* what he thought. Instead, she said, "Jed, I told Stephen you're really a P.I. I saw no reason to keep on pretending. In fact, I had to tell him for, um, personal reasons."

Stephen's eyes narrowed as Ashley spoke. He was observing her closely, as if studying an ancient urn. And then he looked at Jed. Stephen opened his mouth once, but closed it before saying anything. Rising, he held out his hand. "Let's you and I begin all over again, shall we?"

Jed dumped the bundle of folders onto the table and shook the other man's hand. He cleared his throat. "Sorry about last night, Mather. The truth is, I wanted to check you out. I called the University of Chicago's Oriental Institute this morning and told them I was a science reporter for *National Geographic*. They were happy to supply me with your itinerary and validate your current research." Jed's smile was thin, his voice flat.

"Funny, I have a feeling I should be researching *you*, Wyatt. Ashley says she doesn't want the police involved. Not to cast any aspersions on your ability, but I hope that's not a serious mistake."

Jed gave Stephen a deadly look. The archaeologist stepped back a pace. "She can call the police any time she feels I can't get the job done," Jed said. "Since I'm still on the job, I called a locksmith this morning. You'll have to turn in your room key."

Dammit, Jed thought. He still had a funny feeling about Stephen. After all, it was possible to hire local talent long distance. Even sadistic deviant talent. A muscle jumped in Jed's cheek. In fact, being in the Jordan Valley made a damn good alibi for Mather.

And then Jed told himself he was letting an overactive imagination get the better of him. Not to mention an overactive jealousy gland that kicked in whenever the professor got within touching distance of Ashley.

Jed glanced again at the ring, its winking facets mocking him. If Ashley put on that ring, he'd get the hell out of her life as soon as he could. If she didn't . . .

Stephen's face reddened when he saw what Jed was staring at. He snatched up the ring without looking at anyone. "I have to supervise the uncrating of our findings from the dig, Ashley. Among other things, we unearthed a hot tub from an ancient brothel. Seems like the pull between the sexes is nothing new," he added dryly, dropping the ring in his pocket. "See you later. And please try to give some thought to what we discussed last night." His expression was pained. "And be assured that I'll do my best to protect you. I'm nothing if not persistent. As you well know." Aiming a meaningful look at Jed, he left.

Jed's heart did a cartwheel the instant the diamond disappeared into Stephen's pocket. As soon as the door closed, he hauled Ashley out of the chair and into his arms, kissing her full on the mouth.

When he came up for air, he said, "Marry me. Come live with me in New York and marry me. Today. We'll get blood tests this afternoon. I won't even ask if you slept with him last night."

Ashley blinked, feeling as if Jed's words had sucked all the breath out of her. Was this just another ploy to get her in bed?

She wriggled out of his arms. "You! You're insufferable! I don't need your damn magnanimity. It's none of your business what I did last night. You've made it quite clear you want a relationship that's strictly without ties or a future."

She stalked away from him, then whirled back around. "How dare you say you'll marry me now. *After* you see an engagement ring from another man! Do you think I'm some sort of prize you have to wrestle away from the competition?"

Jed raised an eyebrow. It had never occurred to him she wouldn't understand his motives.

"Ashley, listen to me," he said evenly. "I was going to ask you to come with me to New York last night, before Stephen ever even made an appearance. The marriage thing would've evolved from there. As a matter of fact, I intended it to evolve from there."

She was so angry she couldn't have listened to reason if it crawled into her brain. "Don't lie to me! Why don't you sell me a bridge in Brooklyn, too? Just how stupid do you think I am? You think that I won't fall into your arms anymore because of that ring. So you had to up the ante, right?"

Jed stared, mesmerized by the sight of her flushed cheeks, her heaving chest, her dilated eyes. He'd only seen her this aroused . . .

A picture of himself buried deep in Ashley's body swirled in his head, and he went rock hard. He blinked, stumbling back against the wall for support and trying to remind himself that Ashley was mad at him about something. He tried to remember what it was. "Just think about last night. Remember everything that led up to . . . our being together, and you'll see I'm not lying." He snapped his fingers. "Right. I'm not lying. I said I'd never lie to you again, and I damn well meant it. You're jumping to the wrong conclusions. It's five years ago all over again. Just calm down and—"

She shook her head, suddenly seeing beyond her anger, wanting Jed to see, too. "Even worse than what you didn't say, Cooper, is what you did say. Even if you meant the proposal, do you think I could marry you, only to see you sell out? The man I fell in love with was the man driven by his dreams, the man who wanted to help kids like me . . ."

He didn't hear past the word "love."

"Aha! You love me, you just said it. And even though I never said it, I love you, too. I just didn't know it. I mean, I never thought about it in those words, but now that I am, I know I do. I love you.

You love me. Two plus two is four. So start packing."

"What am I going to do with you!"

Jed took a step toward her. "I'll show you," he growled. "I'll show you what works real well with me."

"That was a rhetorical question." Ashley gulped. She wiped a wrist across her brow. "Now let's try a grammar lesson. Listen to the tense of my verbs. Maybe I *fell* in love with you once. And maybe the feeling *was* coming back. But that was before. Before I saw this ... this other manipulative, sex-crazed caveman part of you. You're the best advocate Stephen could've asked for. He has morals, standards, rectitude! Compared to you he's Sir Galahad!"

Jed's eyes narrowed into thin sapphire gleams of male satisfaction. "Uh, princess? Using all my powers of deduction, I think I'm beginning to see the total picture. Stephen Mather, that man of high rectitude and morals, has never slept with you, has he? The pure saintly professor knows nothing about the real you, does he? Not like I do— Hey!"

He threw up a hand and ducked as she threw a handful of jelly beans at him. They hit the wall, clattering like hail.

Ashley felt the heat run through her body, and she wanted to kill him. Her voice dripped acid.

"You're unbelievable. From everything you've told me, you *are* your father's son! He trained you just right!"

"Whoa! No personal insults. Sit down, take that little hand out of the jelly bean jar and—"

"*You* sit down, Cooper." Dismayed at her behavior, she jerked her fingers out of the jar. "Sit down and think about how wrong you are for me. You're the one man in the world who makes me lose control, and I'm sick of it! How dare you do this to me! First of all, the *real* me doesn't jump into bed with someone I barely know. And second, the *real* me isn't a hot-tempered fool!"

Amazingly, he had sat down when she'd ordered him to. Now he said equably, "Maybe it's because you love me, Jamie. That's why I get to you. And that's why you show me the real you. The sooner you admit it, the sooner we'll get everything straightened out, and you can come to New York with me."

"Oh, you, you . . . I loathe . . ."

Unable to get the words out, she ran out the office, slamming the door so hard the stained glass vibrated. Blindly, she dashed upstairs.

At first she didn't even notice the wooden basket overflowing with pink and white carnations at her door. Or the stuffed gray kitten propped in a sitting position in the middle of the flowers. And then she stopped.

The soft plush had been sliced open, and the stuffing was spilling out. It was covered in—Ashley sniffed—ketchup and wearing Smoky's collar. With incredible clarity, she knew what this latest gift meant. The stalker had Smoky.

7

ASHLEY SHRIEKED. Then with shaking hands, she read the note attached to the basket handle with a ribbon:

Roses are red
Violets are blue
This kitten's a symbol
Of what I'll do to you

And then the tears started. Ashley carried the basket into her apartment. She held her hands over her eyes, counting to ten. When she was sure she could speak a whole sentence through, she picked up the phone and called Jed. She wiped her eyes with her knuckles, then with tissues, then with a dish towel. And still the tears came.

Minutes later, Jed returned from disposing of the stalker's latest offering. He was filled with dread. This guy wasn't going to stop until Ashley was dead.

Stop it, he told himself. *You will not think that way. You're going to nail the creep.*

Jed took a step toward Ashley, and she took a step back, her arms folded. He was afraid if he touched her she'd break.

"I'm sorry about Smoky," he said evenly, hoping his calm was contagious. "Most likely, Smoky slipped out of the apartment when Stephen came in. He must've gotten out the street door when I went running last night."

"Or when Stephen left," Ashley said hoarsely, wiping her knuckles over her eyes, the tears still flowing.

Jed nodded. "Whatever. How long have you had Smoky, honey?"

"Four months. Just four months."

"And would you have mentioned him to any of your clients?"

"Maybe. Stuff comes up. Especially with repeat clients. It gets to be more like a social visit sometimes than a business appointment." She sniffled, quietly grateful Jed was allowing her to keep a remnant of dignity by not treating her like a woman in the middle of a nervous breakdown.

"Okay, Ashley, listen." Gently he positioned her next to him on the couch, heartsick at the sight of her chalky complexion.

"Ash, when I burst into your office before, I never got a chance to tell you what I was up to. I saw a clinical psychologist this morning, a woman who does a lot of trial work as an expert witness to these kinds of cases.

"According to her, once this kind of pathological personality kills an animal, it's like stepping over the line. It encourages the guy, gives him a feeling of power. He obviously thinks he won't be caught, which must be why he took Smoky. She also warned me about watching for an escalation in violence."

Jed kept his voice level. "Now, don't worry just because I've given you a worst-case scenario. I'm moving in with you, so the creep will *not* be able to hurt you. Don't even think about arguing with me. I'm—"

"Okay."

"No, I mean it . . . Okay?"

"Yes."

He nodded with relief, having been prepared for an argument. "Good. Our guy—" he waved at Ashley's stained-glass windows "—could be watching from anywhere across the street. There're more high rises and elevator buildings than brownstones on that side of the block. The lake view is on the east, and the city view looks right over your place. I bet he rents an apartment somewhere within telescope range."

He sighed. "You've got windows all over this place, honey. And the long diagonal window that extends across both stories looks onto your staircase and tells him when you leave your apartment and when you come in. Not to mention your office windows. I think that's how he's timing his visits so well."

She nodded, suddenly finding it hard to swallow. "I have a picture of Smoky taken in my office, Jed, on that long slate table—the one with the big tortoise on it?" He nodded. "Any client could've seen it in the last two months and known he was my cat. He even wore that little red collar, in case he ever got out. God, what pervert would kill a kitten? Smoky trusted everyone. He'd go to anyone. . . ."

Jed caressed her cheek. "Hey, Jamieson, I don't have the answers yet. But I swear I'm gonna find them. Can I get you something? A little brandy, a glass of water?"

"Maybe some chocolate candy," she whispered. "There's some in the freezer. I know it sounds crazy, but it helps."

"Okay. I'll be right back."

Jed dumped the chocolate candy on the couch between them. He held up a finger. "First, we take care of your face," he said. Gently, he wiped the tears from her cheeks with a dish towel. Then he handed her a piece of candy.

She ate two at a time, the color slowly seeping back into her cheeks. "Nothing like a good man and chocolate to help you deal with a crisis," she murmured.

"We're going to nail the creep," Jed stated emphatically. "I promise you. I want you to cancel all your appointments today and then visit each of your tenants. Explain who I am—" a corner of his mouth lifted "—the P.I. part, anyway, and tell them I'll be around to question them. Ask them to keep their eyes open, too. And then we're going to go through these files. I want to pull every repeat client you've seen since you got Smoky, and all new clients in the time you've had that picture on display. The red collar's noticeable in the photo?"

Jed slapped a fist on the coffee table at her nod, a lethal glint in his eye. "I also want to check out Amanda Bergman very carefully."

"You think Amanda . . . ?"

"Not Amanda. But she may provide a motive. You've fixed her up with dates more than any other client and apparently she's eventually dumped every one of them. Maybe one of her rejects is blaming you for fixing her up with other men. Like I said before, it might not be a coincidence your place was trashed during your last appointment with her, or that the harassment started after you called her to make that appointment in the first place."

Ashley chewed her lower lip. "And the metronomes were delivered after Amanda's date with Brent Kelly. If someone's watching me, they could be watching her, too."

Jed nodded grimly. "You're getting the hang of this, Ashley. The Amanda connection has a lot of interesting coincidences, and I'm gonna check them out. But don't get excited, it's still speculation." He smiled acidly. "The doctor said to look for someone very normal."

Like Stephen, he told himself, deciding not to share that particular thought just yet. He gritted his teeth, imagining the Stephen possibilities. His hired accomplice could be posing as a client. Or he could've done this last job personally, outraged at finding Ashley with another man.

Ashley interrupted his thoughts. "Jed, that lets out Matt Bartlett, the Vietnam vet. He's definitely not normal."

He sighed, bone weary. "I know. Dr. Cartwright confirmed that he wasn't a likely suspect." He looked at Ashley sharply. "From now on, you don't go anywhere without me. Grocery shopping, clothes shopping, to the cleaners, I'll be right there. And we're going to begin with shutting the creep out of your house. I'd like to cover the office windows, too. It's time to flush him out."

Jed yanked down her Roman shades and started twisting her miniblinds shut.

"No!" she cried. "Don't do that to my cacti. They face the alley, not the front."

"Great. So we force the stalker to peep through the alley window, do we? Why don't you just set up a ladder?"

She merely looked at him with her velvet brown eyes.

Jed raked both hands through his hair. "Okay, okay, stop that. I'll carry the stupid things downstairs and put them in front of the casement windows in the lobby. Plenty of sun there. Agreed?"

"Even the totem-pole cactus that's five feet tall and very delicate and is growing a new arm?"

He rubbed his eyes and sighed. "Yes, even that."

ON HIS FINAL TRIP upstairs, his hands full of cactus spines from transporting the damn things downstairs, Jed kicked open Ashley's apartment door with his foot, his arms full of files. He let out a succinct oath. Stephen was there, a suitcase in his hand.

The archaeologist gave him a hard look. "I'm staying, Wyatt."

Ashley seemed apologetic. "I canceled all my appointments and talked to the tenants like you said. And then Stephen called from the institute to see how I was doing and I, um, told him about our living arrangement."

God, can't you ever lie, Jamieson? Jed dumped the files onto the couch. He turned, arms crossed, taking in the stubborn set of Stephen's small-featured face. Then he relaxed, realizing this was a perfect way to keep an eye on the other man.

Jed nodded curtly. "Join the club, Mather."

They shared takeout pizza for dinner. Jed hardly tasted it, eating by rote. He tried not to grit his teeth when Stephen snuggled up to Ashley on the love seat. Not one wrinkle marred the archaeologist's starched white shirt as he showed off his photos of the dig.

"A real-life Indiana Jones," Jed snorted. He was sprawled on the red couch, wearing his oldest and most faded T-shirt.

Stephen looked up. "No, Wyatt. Indiana Jones is fiction. I deal with reality. And I know who I want to spend the rest of my life with—that's my reality."

Ashley blushed and averted her eyes.

Jed tried not to throw up. He moved farther away from them, making a private enclave for himself and his folders on the couch cushions. Eventually

Stephen's monotonous voice receded into the background as Jed studied Amanda's former dates.

It wasn't until he read the same two files for the fifth time that he got excited. The Amanda connection was sizzling hot. He couldn't take his eyes off the files even while he spoke.

"Ash, what's your opinion of Simon Churchill? And do you really think Harold Bates is absolutely above suspicion?"

Silence. He looked up. Stephen and Ashley were sandwiched together in front of her bedroom door. He hadn't even heard them get up. He squinted. They looked as though they were having a very earnest intimate conversation.

Jed rubbed a hand over his face, shutting his mind to their whispers. With great effort, he reread the files on his two most likely suspects and slapped a third onto the pile. All were tied to Amanda, all repeat clients who could've seen Smoky's photo.

ASHLEY WRIGGLED a little farther away from Stephen, pressing herself against the wall. "No, Stephen," she whispered, increasingly uncomfortable. Stephen was definitely not acting like himself tonight. Jed's presence seemed to be bringing out a new side of him, his tenacious patience turning into something like stubborn obsession. Absurd as the thought was, he was almost . . . frightening.

"No," she reiterated, "I do *not* think it's a good idea for you to share my bedroom. You know how I feel about—"

Stephen aimed a kiss at her lips. He got a mouthful of hair when she turned her head. "I love you. I missed you. We're close to being engaged." He patted his pocket. "Just say yes and put on the ring. I know how to please a woman now, Ashley. I've changed. We can go back to how it was when we were students, remember? Before you—"

Ashley sighed. "I said no, Stephen. If this is the new you, the change isn't for the better. Take a cold shower, then you can sleep in the sun room—the sofa folds out. I'm going to bed."

Before Stephen could protest, his hazel eyes hurt and a little angry, she called out to Jed, telling him that the family-room couch was his. After she showed both men where the linens were, she went into her room, closing the door behind her with a defiant click.

She fell asleep instantly, but it was a troubled sleep. She dreamed she sailed the ocean in a leaky canoe. No land was in sight, and three sharks were circling. One shark wore a tweed blazer, one was half bird, another half cat. A killer whale in a

T-shirt scanned the scene from a distance, while nursery rhymes played in the background.

Ashley was very quiet the next morning, a Sunday. She buried her nose in the newspaper, twirling her hair around her finger, and pretended not to notice the tension in the air.

Jed and Stephen eyed each other warily. Stephen wore neatly creased pants and a bright yellow cabled sweater. Jed wore a rumpled blue T-shirt and never-pressed jeans. Stephen made coffee and toast. Jed made pancakes. Each man asked Ashley if that was okay with her. She absently answered, "Mmm," and continued turning the newspaper pages.

Jed tried to coax a smile out of her. "Hey, Jamieson, here are your pancakes. Special chocolate-chip pancakes." He set a plate down in front of her with a flourish. He'd drawn a smiley face on her pancake with whipped cream.

"You're silly," she said. "But very sweet."

Stephen buttered his toast with heavy slaps of the knife. "Childish," he muttered.

"Imaginative and creat—"

Ashley cut in. "Guys, I have to take a ride today, solo. You can watch me off safely, but I have to go alone."

"No!" they said in unison.

"Why do I feel like I'm under house arrest?"

"It's for your own good," chided Stephen.

"You're not going anywhere alone," stated Jed.

She shook her head. "I swear, this is like being locked up with Laurel and Hardy."

Jed shook his head. "Don't try and throw us on the defensive, kiddo. No going anywhere alone. Except to the bathroom."

"Okay, have it your way. You can follow me."

Stephen eyed Jed and nodded.

Ashley rolled her eyes.

Thirty minutes later, heading northwest on Harlem into suburban Norridge, Jed swore as he cut in front of a silver Mercedes. The distance between his Grand Prix and Ashley's Volvo was growing.

"I'd say she's doing a damn good job of losing us," Stephen said dryly. Suddenly he braced his arm against the dashboard as Jed slammed on the brake and turned sharply into a side street.

"Hell," Jed rasped, "she didn't even use a turn signal! Now what?"

Jed followed Ashley to a strip mall, where she entered a florist shop without giving them a backward glance.

The men sat in strained silence until Stephen spoke. "She really gets to you, doesn't she, Wyatt?"

Jed gave a curt nod. "That she does. It's my responsibility to protect the lady, and I take that responsibility seriously."

"I can see that. I think I'm beginning to see a lot, actually."

Jed glanced at him, then away. "She's coming out," he said. "We're off." Tires squealing, he followed Ashley into Merrymount Cemetery, understanding finally dawning. "Her parents. She's going to see her parents." He paused. "Let's see, the accident was during winter break when Sean was staying with her, so this must be one of their birthdays or something."

Stephen gave him a long look, tapping his nose. "This is curious. In the seven years I've known her, Ashley hasn't mentioned her parents in more than passing conversation. You seem to know quite a bit, however. I know they died when she was in her teens . . ."

"Fourteen." Jed bit off the word. "She was fourteen and in high school when they died. She went through a hell of a lot. Did you know a SOB of a social worker threw her in an abusive foster home until Sean bailed her out? Fortunately Sean was able to hire an attorney specializing in children's rights."

Stephen sat up straight. "I suppose you think you know everything there is to know about Ashley."

"Try me."

"What was Ashley's major in college?"

"Communications."

"What's her favorite food?"

"Anything chocolate."

"What's her favorite pastime?"

"Filling in her calendar. And going to movies and musicals. And don't forget how she takes her coffee and tea—with a pound of sugar."

Stephen's face was flushed. "Okay, Wyatt," he huffed, "you've made your point. I'm sure your credentials are good, but leave Ashley to me. In terminology you might understand—back off."

"Gotcha, professor," Jed drawled. He grinned irreverently. "As long as Ashley wants me to, that is."

Before Stephen could reply, Jed's eyes narrowed. "She's pulling into that parking area. Let's go."

Both men got out of the car, but kept their distance as Ashley threaded her way through the grounds. She was headed toward a double marker of gray marble.

Jed held out an arm to bar Stephen from getting any closer as Ashley knelt, setting the flowers down. He could tell he'd more than riled the archaeologist, who was breathing like a bull facing a red cape. When Stephen finally seemed to calm himself, Jed removed his arm and wearily leaned against a huge oak.

Stephen took that opportunity to bolt toward Ashley. She winced as he put an arm around her.

"Ashley, why didn't you ever tell me anything about your parents? Why did you tell him?" Stephen jerked his head in Jed's direction.

Ashley shrugged his arm off her shoulders. "Stephen, not now. Give me a few minutes. Please."

Stephen's eyes seemed to glitter with anger. She'd never seen him angry before, she realized. For seven years, he'd been as comfortable to have around as an old chenille robe, and not once had she seen him lose his temper.

He waved his hands wildly. "Oh, I suppose I should wait like your faithful shadow over there. Well, you try waiting seven years, Ashley. Only to find out some stranger knows more about your girlfriend than you do! Give me your keys. I'll see you back at the apartment."

He grabbed the key ring from her fingers and spun on his heel, a little spurt of gravel flying up under his well-polished shoe.

Ashley thrust out a hand to stop him, then dropped it. What could she say? That she'd had a one-night stand with the stranger? That the one-night stand wanted to marry her? She believed Jed now. About everything. The arrogant, misguided, very sweet and very concerned Jed Wyatt Cooper loved her.

She sighed. But that still didn't mean two plus two always made four.

And then she sensed Jed was right behind her. In his well-worn shoes, he'd been able to sneak up on her. Very gently he put his hands on her shoulders. His lips touched her ear, sending quivers over her scalp. She could smell his soapy scent. "Take your time, Ash. Do what you have to do," he murmured. Then he moved away.

She stood beside her parents' graves for half an hour. Finally she almost felt normal. She turned around and looked at Jed. "I come here every year on their anniversary."

He hitched his fingers in his pockets, straining with the effort not to touch her again. "You miss them, don't you?"

She nodded. "It's still hard to believe they won't be back from a buying trip one day. It's hard when you don't get a chance to say goodbye."

"But you don't have to miss *me*, Ash. You don't have to tell me goodbye."

Jed's voice was whiskey rough. He reached out to skim a breeze-blown curl off her cheek.

She shook her head. "I'm not in the mood for riddles, Jed. Stephen's waiting for us at the brownstone. And I suspect you might've said something that put him in a very bad mood."

"*Moi?*"

They ambled back to the car, bodies close but not quite touching.

ALL THREE GRANDFATHER clocks read 12:00 a.m.

Jed twisted and turned on the couch, punching his pillow into lumpy shapes. Finally he tossed it away. Sweeping his arm across the floor, he caught hold of his duffel bag. He dragged out the package of cigarettes and matches he'd thrown in for just such an occasion. Somehow he'd guessed Ashley would revive bad habits.

Jed lit up and took a deep drag. The last time he'd smoked had been five years ago—after Ash had thrown him out of her life.

Jed laid his head back against a curled elbow. It had been a long day. The roommates had been virtually silent during Chinese take-out dinner, letting the TV keep them company. After eating, they'd sipped brandy and taken turns reading every last section of the Sunday *Tribune* and *Sun-Times*. Eventually they'd bid each other good-night with exaggerated yawns and stretches.

Restless, Jed smoked another cigarette, then lit a third. As if counting sheep, he began to envision a soothing scenario, one he'd been picturing for the past year. It often came to him just before sleep. He saw himself reconciling with his father, the prodigal son welcomed home.

Jed took a deep drag on his cigarette, still not soothed. Instead, he began to see his happy ending in a new light.

He saw himself reviving a career he detested. He saw himself winning an acceptance that was doled out conditionally. And he saw himself living a lie. Why hadn't he realized that before? Had it taken a certain little redhead to change his perspective? With a small grunt of disgust, Jed ground his cigarette into an ashtray.

He was staring at the ceiling, hands under his head, when a figure padded into the kitchen, opposite the family room. Through slitted eyes, he saw Ashley stop and study his still form, obviously assuming he was sleeping.

She flipped on the overhead oven light and opened the freezer.

Jed squinted, the small light illuminating her as if she were on stage. She spooned chocolate-chip ice cream into a bowl, covered it with syrup and spooned half a jarful of maraschino cherries on top. In minutes she'd devoured the whole thing.

"Ten million calories, easy," Jed whispered as she placed the bowl in the sink.

She whirled around. "You were watching me!"

"Yup," he said agreeably. "For such a little thing, you sure know how to eat."

"I have a high metabolism. Besides, I couldn't sleep." She walked toward him, tugging her chenille robe more tightly around her. "Neither could you apparently. I thought I smelled cigarettes. I didn't know you smoked."

"Last time was five years ago."

She shivered at the desire in his voice. "I, um, have to go to sleep. Right away."

"Sorry, Jamieson. But I have to do this." She didn't even get a chance to blink. He was off the couch in a blur, and suddenly she was in his arms. His lips found hers in a heart-stopping kiss.

"No more thinking, Ash. Just you and me. Doing what's right for us. And you know this is right." He nibbled her neck all the way down to the V of her robe. Then his hand stole inside to cup one full breast through her clingy satin gown.

Ashley was spellbound by Wyatt's kisses, his warm hands on her body, his tobacco scent. She fumbled at his jeans. Experimentally she stroked him, her touch first hard, then soft, and he shuddered, sending a thrill through her body.

She stopped abruptly, filled with doubt. She whispered, "Stephen will—"

"Shh. He won't. He had four brandies to our one. He'll sleep all night."

She felt as if she was in a steam room, drowning in heavy languorous air. "Yes," she breathed. "Yes." She tugged off his jeans. She couldn't ignore the truth anymore. She loved him, dammit. She loved him and she wanted him. That couldn't be wrong. As of that minute, she knew her relationship with Stephen was over.

Jed picked her up and deposited her on the couch. In one swift movement, he slid her gown off, drawing in a breath at the sight of her ivory body, bathed by moonlight. "Oh, my God, you're gorgeous. I thought it was my memory..."

Jed bent his head to suckle her breasts, sending hot ripples through her midsection. Then, without her having to ask for more, he slipped lower and buried his head in her soft curls, drinking from her until she was moving rhythmically, spasmodically.

She was frightened and exhilarated and out of her head with desire. Then Jed's fingers followed his mouth, and she exploded in a wild release, amazed that she had lost control so quickly. She breathed rapidly, shallowly, her whole body flushed.

He bent his head and kissed her between her thighs. "My wild little tiger. I was right before, wasn't I? There's been no one else."

"No one else," she echoed, feeling like a piece of very hot putty in very skillful hands.

Raised on his elbows, Jed held his body over hers, staring at her body so soft and melting in the moonlight. With a surge of satisfaction, he lowered himself on top of her, and she wrapped her arms around him. He pushed against her, so hard and swollen it hurt, wanting to make it good for her all over again. He promised himself she would always remember tonight.

Cupping his hands under her bottom, he half lifted her onto his erection. He made teasing shallow thrusts, bringing her to the brink slowly. Using more control than he'd thought he possessed, he held himself back, not letting his climax happen until she was ready. He let her confidence build, allowing her natural passion to take over.

Ashley felt so hot—it was happening all over again, that soaring rocking-horse ride to the peak, but fuller, deeper, richer. This time she wanted him to share, she wanted to feel him deep inside her. "Now, Jed," she moaned. "Come with me this time. Please."

"I thought you'd never ask."

He scraped her nipple with his teeth and her bottom bucked under his hands. "That pleases you?" He nibbled her other breast, and she bucked again. "Ah, yes." He slid in more deeply, his hands opening her thighs, before he teasingly pulled out.

Lovingly, his mouth closed around a rosy areola, and she convulsed, wrapping her arms and legs tight around his hard body.

"Don't tease a lady," she murmured.

"Never." Heart thumping, sweat beading his body like rain, Jed reached down, searching for his duffel bag and tugging out a condom.

It wasn't right, he told himself, sliding on the sheath. She deserved slow magic and sweet words. But he wasn't in a place where he could give her anything slow or sweet.

He entered her swiftly, fiercely, deeply, all teasing cast aside. She grunted once at the fullness of him and then her legs swiftly were around his hips. Within moments their bodies found a rhythm, and they gave themselves up to it.

It was wonderful. A pulsating rush that threatened to drive Ashley mad. And still Jed urged her on, until they reached the peak and tumbled crazily over the edge.

When he could breathe again, Jed turned her on her side to face him. Tossing an afghan over their bodies, he wrapped his arms around her. "I'm sorry. I shouldn't have done that here, on the couch, in secret, like a teenager in heat. If you're mad at me, I understand."

He nuzzled the moist flesh of her neck. "I love you. I want us to be together forever. But I'll leave if you want after I catch the creep."

Ashley snuggled against Jed's chest. He was making her temperature shoot up again. Wild licks of fire ignited through her body. *Again. Again. Again!* She lowered one hand to feel his growing hardness, stroking him until he wouldn't be able to stop what was going to happen. What she was going to *make* happen. "Again," she murmured. "Love me again and the hell with everything else. The world is you and me and this couch."

She nipped his flat nipples, tasting the salt. Growing bolder, she kneaded his erection slowly, teasingly, quickly learning how to make him groan with pleasure with a light stroke here, a firm pressure there.

With a shudder, Jed grabbed her hand, murmuring something about fast learners.

He covered her with his hard body, tucking her underneath him, purring, "I love you, Jamie," over and over while they came together again.

Hours later, Ashley's eyes snapped open. It was growing light. She looked across the room at a grandfather clock and panicked. Stephen couldn't find her in Jed's arms. She was going to tell him, but it would be cruel if he found out this way. Jed was still asleep, dark curling lashes feathering his cheeks and tousled hair falling over his brow like a boy's.

She smiled. This was no boy. She kissed his nose, and one eye opened. "You're leaving me?" he murmured.

She grabbed her robe, slipping it over her shoulders, snatching up all evidence of the night's activity. "I have to," she whispered. "Ste—"

"—phen," Jed finished with a sigh. "Last night I made some major decisions. About us. About getting married and staying here in Chicago. If you'll . . ."

There was a thump from the sun room, then footsteps. Ashley bent down and kissed Jed on the mouth. "I love you dearly, Cooper," she whispered.

And then she was gone, her scent lingering in the air.

8

By the time Ashley emerged from her bedroom, showered and dressed, Stephen was awake and Jed was gone. A cryptic message was scrawled on a napkin. "Chasing down some leads," it read. "Keep the faith. Wyatt."

Her heart sank. God, was last night a dream, a crazy sex-filled hallucination? She looked at the couch, an ordinary red couch with a carelessly folded blanket tossed over one arm.

Under Stephen's curious gaze, Ashley made coffee and scrambled eggs. She hoped he didn't notice her face turning crimson with the memory of what had happened on that couch.

"Philip Marlowe dashed out early this morning on some sort of secret mission," Stephen commented sarcastically. "A section of the *Tribune* was rolled up in that scruffy leather jacket he wears. Before he left, he also hired two off-duty policemen as bodyguards. One's outside the door now, and the other takes over at night. And he ordered me to sit in the lobby and play guard, too. Which, of course, I'll be happy to do . . . for you."

Ashley smiled brightly, despite her confusion. She couldn't help but wonder why Jed felt she needed a guard when Stephen was here.

Before she left for her office, she made a lunch date with Stephen at a popular neighborhood deli, the kind of place that was always crowded. For what she had to say, she wanted noise and bustle. A carnival would have been nice.

The morning sped by much too fast. At noon sharp, she and Stephen slid into a leather booth, her hired shadow nodding matter-of-factly at them from across the room. Stephen straightened his white turtleneck and ordered a corned beef sandwich on rye and a chocolate shake.

"I'll have the same," Ashley said wanly. She bit a nail. Where the dickens was Jed? Had he disappeared so mysteriously because of last night? Because of second thoughts?

"We left Sherlock a note, Ashley," Stephen grumbled. "You can stop checking your watch. Assuming he can read, he'll understand. I certainly can't imagine what sort of leads he thinks he's going to find in that newspaper."

Before she could defend Jed, Stephen held up a hand and said, "Ashley, I want to apologize for upsetting you yesterday at the cemetery. I'm sorry. Really, really sorry. There's just something about that man that sets my teeth on edge. The way he looks at you . . ."

"I know, Stephen."

"You know?"

"Yes. He looks at me as if . . . as if we mean something to each other."

Stephen swallowed. "You accept that, Ashley? That sort of . . . intimacy?"

"I have to explain something to you, Stephen."

"And you asked me to lunch in order to explain that something?"

She nodded miserably.

"You're not going to accept my ring, are you? And this has something to do with Sam Spade, doesn't it?"

Ashley spoke as gently as she could. "Stephen, do you remember when we broke up five years ago and I told you I'd met someone during the time we weren't seeing each other? That the relationship was brief, and, um, intense, but it went nowhere and left me hurt and confused."

"Yes, I remember. All the fire went out of our relationship after that."

They paused as their order came. Ashley nibbled on a french fry and then took an inordinate amount of time smearing mustard on her bread. She didn't even like mustard.

Stephen halfheartedly took a bite out of a bulging sandwich. A second passed, then he gaped at Ashley, and his food went down in one gulp. "You can't possibly mean that he's . . . ?"

She nodded. "Yes."

She flinched as Stephen hit the table with his fist. Immediately he apologized. "Sorry, go on."

She swallowed. "Jed's the man I met five years ago. By a very strange coincidence he's back here working undercover. I would have told you sooner, but I had to, uh, get things straight in my own mind first."

She looked away from Stephen's tight face. "You see, you were right. Jed's not what he seems. He's an accomplished writer and an attorney and a million other things, as well. The P.I. identity's just one of many." She dropped her eyes, pleating her napkin.

"Stephen, I know it's a terrible cliché, but I think you and I were meant to be friends, not lovers. That's what we're best at." She gave him a sick smile and started tying her straw wrapper into tiny knots.

Stephen stared at her, his hazel eyes dark and still. "All I wanted was for us to get back to how it was in the beginning, before... But now, of course, it all makes sense." His voice cracked, and he buried his face in his hands.

She felt as if she'd kicked a puppy.

After a minute, Stephen cleared his throat. "Ashley, I know this may sound a trifle strange coming from me, but Wyatt, or whatever the heck his name is, seems to know you very well. Perhaps—" he coughed "—better than I do. Maybe he'll make you happy in a way I couldn't. And that's the reason I'm going to let you walk away."

She reached a hand out to him. "Stephen . . ."

He shook his head. "There's nothing more to say."

They both dropped their heads and pretended to eat, trying to make small talk. Stephen insisted he'd take guard duty again until Jed got back. "I still care about you, Ashley. And I can still be your friend. Isn't that what you wanted?"

Filled with a strange bittersweet feeling, she let Stephen pay the check and escort her home.

Miss Stabe's face was stained red with the fury of a tantrum. She ripped the heavy telescope off its mounting and threw it to the floor, her wig going askew with the effort.

Breathing hard and scanning her apartment, empty but for the card table and chairs and shopping bags lining the walls, Miss Stabe upended the table and chairs. Then she savagely dumped the contents of each bag onto the floor. Magazines, tape recorders, rubber gloves, a pair of glasses, wigs, makeup and handcuffs tumbled out with a clatter.

"I'll show them!" she cried, kicking the spilled contents across the room like so many soccer balls.

Her curly blond wig went more askew with each kick. "Think, think, *think!*"

"You can't see into the deceitful witch's apartment anymore. A blond man's stationed in the lobby and a fat man in an ill-fitting suit has been pacing the grounds all morning. So think, Miss Stabe. Think. What would your partner do?"

Miss Stabe sneezed violently, and her wig finally fell off completely. She stared at the blond curls lying on the floor and shrieked, "I've been decapitated!"

And then a gleeful smile spread over her face.

She minced into the bathroom, and using cold cream, she scrubbed every trace of makeup from her face.

A man in a dress walked out of the bathroom. He retrieved the wig from the floor and held it aloft, speaking to it. "My dear Miss Stabe, I think your partner would make his final move now. In fact, I'll ask him." The man squeezed his eyes shut and wrinkled his brow, deep in concentration. After a minute, his soft brown eyes popped open. "He told me he's going for it in the very near future."

Giggling, he let the wig slip from his fingers into a wastebasket. "I think this is goodbye, Miss Stabe. I won't be needing you anymore."

As he left the apartment, the man recited a nursery rhyme in a rhythmic chant. It was "Humpty Dumpty."

BY THE TIME Ashley finished with her last client, she was weary and out of sorts. Charity True, shaped like a pumpkin and possessing a mane of cheerleader hair, had complained nonstop about every potential date Ashley had shown her. She finally chose a divorced doctor, although she whined that he was bald and only a pediatrician. Ashley had bitten her tongue more than once.

On her way out of the office, Ashley smoothed her long denim skirt and straightened her matching blazer, feeling less than wonderful. *Jilted, jilted, jilted*, kept flashing through her mind like a blinking neon sign. Then she glanced around the lobby and realized Stephen was nowhere in sight. Wryly she told herself that yesterday she'd had two men pursuing her. Now they'd both vanished. Her footsteps echoing on the stairs to her apartment, she couldn't help noticing the first floor was very still.

Ashley fumbled with her new lock, which was sticky and recalcitrant.

She swung her apartment door open at last, and her heart skipped a beat.

Jed was waiting for her, sprawled on the love-seat. He whipped his arms behind his back the minute she stepped through the door.

"Ah, the prodigal returns," she quipped.

She stood rooted to the spot, not sure what came next, except for a strong feeling that she was about to find out if last night's magic was mutual—or one big embarrassing misunderstanding.

Jed nodded at the cushion next to him. "Sit down and close your eyes."

"I'm not in the mood for games, Cooper. I think we need to— Was that a squeal?"

"Neither am I, Jamieson, and we don't. My shoes squeak. Now shut up and sit down and trust me for once in your life."

She gulped and sat, closing her eyes. Was he about to let her down gently? Would she be on the receiving end of the speech she'd used that very afternoon? *Let's be friends, Ashley. Last night was a mistake.*

Something small was placed in her lap. Then Jed took her hand and put it on the lump. It had sharp little needles that dug into her knees and was very soft. She opened her eyes and gasped.

"Do you like him? It took me the whole damn day to search the classifieds for a pure gray kitten with little gold eyes. Oh, Ashley, don't cry. Hell, maybe I should've gotten you an orange tabby. I thought we'd call him Dusty."

She wiped an eye, scanning the floor. "You put out Smoky's toys for him and some food. Dusty sounds good." She shook her head. "I don't know what to say. This is the most thoughtful, wonderful..."

She rubbed her cheek against the drowsy kitten's fuzzy coat. "Last night really happened? We shared the same...dream?"

"Does this feel familiar, Jamieson?" Jed lowered his mouth over hers, his tongue tasting her lips, then parting them and confidently exploring her mouth.

"I can see it's familiar," he said huskily. "You have the sexiest look in your eyes. If your dream was anything like mine, it was way up there."

She grinned. "Did the earth move?"

"There was a definite new tilt to its axis." Suddenly his expression turned serious. "The rest was real, too. Do you remember my telling you about a friend from law school who's been after me to hook up with him? Last Christmas, Ed told me about a case, a complaint against a fast-food place that banned someone from buying a homeless man a hamburger, for cripe's sake. I was as jealous as hell."

Jed's eyes gleamed with an intense light while he talked about his friend's practice. It was that crusader look Ashley remembered well from five years ago when he'd told her how different he was from his father. A topic, she suddenly realized, he seemed to be deftly avoiding.

"... and the new clinic's partially funded by a local bar association," Jed was saying, "and Ed wants me in it. It's the kind of thing I can really sink my teeth into." He took a deep breath. "I'm going to accept his offer."

He nibbled her neck, his kisses burning like hot coals. "I also want to sink my teeth into this tender flesh, of course."

Ashley could swear the room temperature rose to that of a small sun. Her voice came out in a croak. "You're gonna be the best defense the defenseless ever had, counselor. And if you're hungry, I can fix you a tuna-salad sandwich."

Jed looked down at Ashley, dragging his fingers through that shower of russet, inhaling her sweet cut-grass scent. Jeez, he wanted to see that hair spread over his pillow, and then he'd bury himself in that beautiful body without worrying about—

"Stephen," he said flatly. "What about the faithful archaeologist? When I relieved him from guard duty, he walked off into the sunset without even insulting me. Is he sick?"

"I talked to Stephen already. He took it well—all things considered."

Jed's eyes gleamed wickedly. "So, the only thing standing between thee and me is a stalker, hmm?"

"That, and maybe your father, Jed," she said lightly. "Is this something we need to discuss?"

Jed's jaw tightened. "You are one perceptive redhead, Jamieson. Why don't you make those sandwiches and then we'll talk."

Ashley gave him a thoughtful look and nodded. "It's a date, Cooper."

JED SET A MATCH to a small pine log in the fireplace, waiting for the satisfying snap of dry wood igniting. It was a brittle fall day, a good day for a fire. He closed the iron screen over the flames, staring thoughtfully at the red and orange tongues of light.

Ashley set their sandwiches on the kitchen table. She took a few steps toward Jed and got right to the point. "I think it's very important for you and your father to reconcile now. But you—you don't think being an under six-figures attorney defending the needy is going to exactly cut it in his eyes, do you?"

Jed let out a short burst of genuine laughter. "Hell, no! Bryant Cooper, senior partner of Cooper, Armstrong and Baker, would laugh himself silly over this. He'd think I was squandering a perfectly good law degree."

Restlessly Jed prowled the room. "Ash, that's not my problem anymore. The way I see it, it's his. I will see him and try to reconcile. After we're married and settled. I promise." He grinned slyly. "How the hell can he resist seeing his four adorable redheaded granddaughters one day?"

"Four!" she squeaked, stumbling backward into the couch.

Jed grinned. "It's true. I'd like four little girls just like you."

With two easy strides he was at her side, pulling her to his chest and burying his fingers in her curls.

"Jeez, honey, you need to relax. You're so stiff. We can't map out our entire future in the next hour. Let's let it unfold . . . spontaneously." He massaged her shoulders until he felt the tension leave her body. "That's better. You have to learn to believe in the future, to believe in me. Try being more like Dusty."

Ashley followed his gaze to the kitten curled in a loose ball on a window seat.

"Like this, you mean?" Contentedly she leaned into his hard chest, breathing in his lime scent. *Just don't get too happy,* a sneaky little voice whispered.

She ignored the voice. "Should I purr?"

"That's the idea." Jed snapped his fingers and disappeared into the bathroom, coming back with a brush. "I'm gonna make you purr. C'mere."

He sat lengthwise on the couch, drawing her back into the V of his long corded legs. "Now, just relax."

With slow lazy strokes, he brushed her hair. It responded like a living creature, waving, crackling and shimmering in the fire's glow. Jed filtered a handful of curls through his fingers, like so many glittery gems. "I want to make you happy. I want you to trust me to do that always."

Ashley's muscles and bones seemed to melt at his touch. Leaning back, she sighed with satisfaction, almost ready to believe that they could have a perfect life together.

Jed added a kiss with each stroke, sending tingles down her scalp and goose bumps up and down her body. Suddenly she was no longer relaxed.

One stroke, and Jed nibbled her ear. Another, and he slipped off her jacket, tugging down her shirt and kissing her nape. "You taste so damn good."

He threw the brush down. "I'm famished. Not for tuna. I have to taste you all over." There was a catch to his voice, and in moments the room was an enchanted place, lit only by fire.

"Lift up your hands," he ordered as he pulled off her gold top. With one smooth movement he'd removed her lacy bra and was cupping her breasts from behind. She leaned back, her own fire igniting.

His skilled fingers teased her nipples into tender aching nubs while he planted kisses on her neck. "Now lift up just a little . . . on your knees. Yes . . ."

He pulled down her skirt, then her panty hose. "Don't turn around," he commanded.

Her heart was beating hammer fast as he took off her skirt and hose. "Mmm," she murmured, suddenly aware of his fingers inching their way into her panties, finding her tender secrets and starting her on an insidious rhythm.

She was moving with his fingers now, slick and wet. She heard him yank down his zipper, drag at his jeans and briefs. Gently his free hand pushed down at the nape of her neck until she was balancing on her hands and knees, trembling and breathing hard.

"Oh, you're so hot, honey," he murmured. He moved his body atop hers, his arousal brushing provocatively between her thighs and against her panties.

She caught her breath, and then in an innate response she slid back and forth against him, feeling him harden with each silken stroke. He was right. She was so hot she was burning up. He nipped the waistband of her panties with his teeth, drawing them down to her knees.

"Put out the fire, Jed."

And then he was inside her.

She pushed back into him, sensitized to an exquisite point like none she'd ever been to before. With each hard plunge of his body she came closer to the peak, but she wanted more. So arching her body, she greedily took him deeper inside.

Then she was out of control, ripples of sweet heat shooting through her body.

"Oh, baby," Jed crooned as he climaxed, fulfilling all her needs.

They collapsed in a sated heap. After a few minutes, Jed spooned Ashley into his side and whispered in her ear, "I've never felt this way with anyone else, Jamie. Making love, not sex."

"But the sex part isn't bad, either."

"You're a wanton creature, Jamieson."

For a while they lay together, watching the shadows grow on the walls as the fire died, shrinking into embers.

Much later, she turned around, putting her hands up under his T-shirt to play with his chest hair.

"We didn't use any protection."

He gave her a sly grin. "The sooner you bear my first daughter, the better. That's how sure I am about us." He cupped her face and began to massage the skin behind her ears. "Somehow, I felt...I felt that you wanted what I wanted," he admitted quietly. "Was I arrogant and smug all over again?"

"Yes, extremely smug and arrogant. But I love you, anyway. And I want to have your baby." She gulped. "Babies. So just once you're excused."

Then Ashley threw away all her caution. "Actually I want them as soon as possible. Maybe twins for starters. Did you know for twins you have to make love twice? It's a genetic fact."

He laughed. "Did you fail Biology 101, honey?"

"Shut up." She ran a fingernail down his chest. "This time I think we should take it very slow, to be sure we get it right."

She pulled off his T-shirt.

Feeling very playful, she moved her hands lower and found him already aroused. She caressed him, all silk and steel, feeling him grow harder.

He groaned. "That definitely won't get you slow."

He stood, hauling her upright with him, a feral glint in his eyes.

She let out a whoop of laughter as Jed lifted her up and carried her into the bedroom.

He tossed her onto the bright Mayan-patterned comforter. "Now we're gonna slow-dance."

He kissed the soft curls in between her legs, kissed her until she didn't know where the kisses left off and her own wetness began.

He dipped inside with one finger, two fingers, and she rode him in a gentle rhythm, starting the wondrous cycle all over again.

Straddling her, Jed rubbed himself between her thighs until she couldn't stand it anymore. She reached out to him, whispering, "Come to me, Jed. *Now.*"

Eyes full of desire, he clasped her arms and pulled her up until they were facing each other. Nibbling on her throat, he said, "Slow and delicious this time. Just like you ordered."

Clenching her earlobe between his teeth, he rose slightly, lifting her bottom with his palms, and then he eased into her with one slow smooth thrust. Deliberately he pulled back, but before she could protest he entered her again. Over and over he thrust into her, slow and deliberate and teasing, until she couldn't stand it any longer.

Suddenly she tugged him closer, her fingers digging into his back. "Now I've got you trapped." She felt him shudder as she increased her demands. They rocked together, their rhythm no longer slow.

Within moments, they reached the pinnacle, and then together they fell over the edge.

As he struggled to regain his breath, Jed realized that for the first time he knew what it meant to love someone. And he understood how one person could give up his life for someone else.

It wasn't until after she'd fallen asleep that Jed reminded himself the stalker was still in the picture. Protectively he tightened his arms around Ashley. He hoped to God he hadn't put her in danger by delaying his investigation for even one day.

9

JED CUPPED his hands against a light breeze and lit a cigarette. He leaned back against the lilac bush, trying to shake off the feeling of dread that had been dogging him ever since he'd woken up that morning. It was a companion to the worry that had nagged him last night, a gut instinct telling him not to relax until the stalker was history.

Jed sighed. Even though Patrick Callahan, a burly seasoned police-force veteran, was on duty, that didn't allow him to breathe easily. It also wasn't enough that he was somewhat skilled himself or that he had access to all the latest crime-busting technology. Maybe nothing was enough when you were dealing with a very clever creep in a very big city.

The phone calls had stopped as soon as he'd set up the tap. It was as if the guy was watching and anticipating Jed's every move. A chess master. Jed raked a hand through his hair. He was probably too smart to use his own phone, anyway, but a phone record from a booth would at least have placed the area of the call. They could even lift prints from a booth. "Wishful thinking," he muttered. "The creep obviously wears gloves."

He took another drag on the cigarette and squinted across the street at brick elevator buildings and sleek glass high rises. The stalker could have a telescope in any one of those windows. *Especially the high rise directly across the street.*

Jed made a sound of disgust. On top of everything else he'd discovered the bastard was using disguises. He'd spent the early morning hours questioning the tenants. The orthodontist's office manager, Helen, had described the "deliveryman" who'd brought the stuffed kitten. She'd seen him walk upstairs with a basket. He had straight black hair, a medium build, a mustache and had sneezed profusely.

That description was no one Ashley could identify. It was also no one Helen could pick out from the photos of Jed's three top suspects. They were the three men Amanda had rejected in the past two months. And that, Jed told himself wearily, was still all he had to go on, even after combing through files until he couldn't see straight.

Jed crushed his last cigarette under his foot, swearing softly. He'd checked out the UPS deliveryman, too. He at least had been for real. The box of metronomes had originally been dropped off at the area UPS office. The clerk had told Jed the customer was of medium height and stocky, with curly brown hair and glasses. The only other relevant detail the clerk could remember was that he'd had a cold. He'd even signed with an obvious pseudonym—John Smith.

Jed admired the psycho's creativity. It was apparent that he'd bulked up with padding, used wigs, mustache, glasses. The UPS clerk couldn't identify the man from the three photos any more than Helen could. Neither could the doorman at the high rise across the street. Just as discouraging, neither the name John Smith, nor the names of the men in the photos, matched the apartment's list of tenants, according to the doorman.

"Simon Churchill," Jed growled in disgust. "Tanner Magill. Harold Bates. One of you is very, very clever and very, very sick."

Jed gritted his teeth. He'd just come from the library, where he'd done a little research. An article in *American Psychology*—a chilling case history of an obsessive gymnastics coach who'd killed one of his athletes—had been particularly illuminating. "The stalker appears very normal," it had said. "The stalker has a compartment of his life he shares with no one. Just his victim.... Ninety percent of stalkers suffer from mental disorders. The stalker sees a rejection and blows it out of proportion."

That last bit of information probably let Stephen out. Any anger he bore Ashley was very acceptable, considering his seven years' worth of unrequited love. A stalker's "love" was based only on illusion and delusion.

Deciding on his next course of action, Jed headed for the car. It was time to pay three particular guys a visit.

Jed eased the Grand Prix into traffic. He told himself that Harold Bates, the owner of a small insurance agency, could make his own hours. And that meant he could easily be spending days glued to a telescope. Ashley had insisted he was wasting his time with Harold, but still . . .

Jed found Bates at his Near North office. A nice place, he thought, eyeing the traditional oak and mahogany furniture, wood paneling and fancy jade chess set on an inlaid wooden table.

Bates trotted out to greet him after Jed queried the receptionist. Jed thought Bates looked friendly and harmless. He shook the little man's hand, explaining he was a P.I. working for Ashley. While he spoke he searched the other man's eyes for any sign of recognition. If Bates was the stalker, he'd have seen Jed around the brownstone.

Harold's mother, who was also his secretary, brought a tray of coffee and homemade brownies into the office, then left. Jed noticed she purposely left the door open a crack, and he bit back a smile.

"I saw Ashley about four weeks ago," Harold said. "She fixed me up with a lovely girl, a school-teacher." Harold sighed. "It was a fiasco. There's only one woman I've ever been comfortable with besides Mother."

Jed filed that information away and politely declined a brownie. "I've told you that Ashley has asked for your cooperation, Mr. Bates, and now I'll tell you why." Jed leaned forward and whispered, "Ashley's being stalked."

Harold's mouth dropped open. "My goodness! What can I do to help, Mr. Wyatt? I know the streets are full of crazies. Do you have any, uh, leads?"

Jed smiled, liking the little man. "No, no leads," he lied smoothly. "I'm just talking to every client Ashley's seen in the past six months. Asking if they'd take a lie-detector test or maybe look at some photos. Routine stuff. And call me Jed."

"Of course, I'd take a lie-detector test. Anything to help Ashley."

Jed felt something furry rub against his leg, and he bent over to pet a yellow cat. "Animal lover?"

Harold sneezed. "My mother's. I'm allergic. To everything. I just touch Satan and my eyes water.

Now if there's anything I can do to help, Mr. Wyatt, er, Jed, you just let me know."

Harold took a big bite of brownie, closing his eyes for a minute of ecstasy. "Delicious, Jed. Mother's brownies are simply divine.

Jed gave Bates a business card.

"Thank you, Jed. Please call me if you have a photo for me to, uh, ID—isn't that what they say in the movies? I'm going to have Mother bake Ashley some brownies. Tell her I'll bring them over tonight."

Harold held out the plate. "Sure you don't want any?"

Amused, Jed shook his head and said goodbye.

Shoving his hands in his pockets, he sauntered down Clark Street toward his car. The street was crammed with glossy storefronts drenched in fall sunshine. "Cross that one off the list," he muttered. "A bumbler like Harold couldn't possibly kill a canary, much less a kitten."

Jed rubbed an index finger across his top lip, wondering what Amanda had seen in Harold. According to Ashley, Amanda was a real looker. Spiffed up and on antihistamines, Harold was probably what women called cute. But he'd still be half a foot shorter than Amanda. Of course, Ashley had said the model had liked Harold's hefty bank account—probably just enough to date him for two months so she could go to Chicago's finest restaurants and clubs.

Jed stopped in front of a southwest gift shop.

He walked out twenty minutes later. He stuffed a huge bag into the car trunk and then wheeled into traffic, concentrating on suspect number two. Simon Churchill was a social worker for a federal agency. Simon had been Amanda's short-lived steady before Harold, and according to Ashley, the relationship had not ended amicably. She hadn't been able to fix him up since.

Jed double-parked in a derelict neighborhood uptown, where the El screeched overhead, swirling garbage and debris under the steel girders. He ambled into the storefront office and perched on the secretary's metal desk, his arms crossed.

"Is Mr. Churchill on his own a lot?" Jed asked casually after identifying himself. The secretary, Miss Marsh, nodded, telling him the caseworkers were often out of the office.

"Has he been out a lot during the past few weeks?" Jed asked, giving the woman a charm-packed grin.

The secretary blushed. "Yes. He's been inspecting a new block of foster homes." Absently weaving a pencil through her pale hair, she lowered her voice and confided, "There do seem to be an awful lot that need checking." She looked ready to tell him more when the street door opened. "Wait a minute, here's Simon now."

Simon Churchill was a good-looking guy, about five-nine, with a mop of sun-bleached hair.

Churchill was cordial until Jed introduced himself. Then reluctantly he invited Jed into his small cubicle, where he called Ashley to verify Jed was on the level, all affability gone. He was even more reluctant to talk after Jed explained the situation.

The blond man tapped a pen on his desk. "Look, Wyatt, you don't have a warrant for my arrest or anything, do you? So I don't have to talk to you at all, much less take a lie-detector test. I'm sorry someone's harassing Ashley, but it sure as hell isn't me. Now if you'll excuse, I have work to do." He grabbed Jed's card and flipped it into the garbage can.

Jed sardonically saluted Churchill. "Thanks for your help, buddy. Oh, and don't bother showing me the door."

Jed stalked out onto the street, sending the pigeons on the sidewalk into a flurry.

Did Churchill have a home to inspect or a telescope to peer through? He scratched behind his ear. He'd definitely struck some kind of nerve. Did it make Churchill feel less like a man to be reminded of the blond bombshell who'd dumped him? Jed remembered how, with a look of distaste, Ashley had told him about Amanda's penchant for "slumming." For fun, Amanda would date guys who were not what she considered worthy.

A social worker would definitely not make big enough bucks for Amanda. He gritted his teeth. If only Churchill had tried to dissemble and act like a man with something to hide.

Jed slid behind the wheel of his car, reaching around the windshield to tear up a parking ticket before he drove off.

He called his last suspect's service from the car phone. Tanner Magill was a self-employed electrician Amanda had dated once between Churchill and Bates. Another slum date, Jed mused cynically. Ashley had told him Magill had been in twice afterward—and he was not a client she looked forward to seeing.

Jed tracked Magill on the North Side. He walked through an elegant bungalow being rebuilt from the inside, maneuvering around sawhorses and loose stacks of lumber. The foreman pointed out a burly man with muscles bulging under a Bears T-shirt.

Jed held out a hand, casually explaining his visit. Just as casually, he cupped his hands and lit a cigarette when Tanner refused to shake.

Magill's gaze narrowed. "I ain't taking no lie-detector test. Is this visit really routine, or is it because of my record? I don't like detectives. I got a problem with authority, ya know?" He grinned slyly. "I had a deprived childhood."

Jed crushed the cigarette out on a twisted piece of scrap metal. All his senses were tingling. "Your record?" he asked evenly. "I told you, I'm just doing a routine check of all the clients Ashley's had in the past six months. Your questionnaire said nothing about a record."

Tucker started his drill, pointing it in front of him like a gun. "Yeah, a record, Mr. P.I., but I don't exactly advertise it. My ex-wife trumped up assault and abuse charges. You know how it is. Women." He raised the drill a little, smiling.

Jed sucked in a breath, forcing himself to keep his head, telling himself this Neanderthal wouldn't be subtle enough to stalk Ashley. Besides, a guy could easily make himself bigger, but there was no way he could make a King Kong physique look medium.

Jed balled his fists in his pockets, filled with disgust. "Maybe I'll be seeing you again, Magill." He took a few steps backward, stopping when Magill turned off the drill.

Jed snapped his fingers. "Oh, yeah." His eyes narrowed, and his voice fell to a growl. "Don't come near Ashley Jamieson or her place again. I'm sure your parole officer would agree with me."

He held Magill's eyes until the man started fiddling with his tools, then turned and left.

Jed hit the sidewalk and sucked in fresh gulps of air. When the sun's warmth had revived him, he tore up his second parking ticket and headed back to Ashley's. He couldn't wait to get there—the hairs on the back of his neck were prickling with a premonition of danger.

He was sure one of the men he'd seen today was the stalker. The question was who.

JED THRUST a Guatemalan patchwork teddy bear into Ashley's arms, determined not to let her see his unease. "For our firstborn. Every child needs a teddy bear."

"You're nuts," she accused teasingly. "What's next? A layette?"

And then Ashley found the bracelet on the bear's arm. "Fetishes!" she whispered, fingering the Indian charm bracelet, which had semiprecious stone fetishes dangling from a sterling silver chain.

Jed's eyes glittered. "Wait for dark, my sweet, and I'll show you what real fetish is." He kissed her ear. "Or maybe I'll show you now."

"Stop it. I've made hamburgers for an early dinner." She took a broiler pan with four misshapen brown balls out of the refrigerator.

"Those are hamburgers?"

"If I'm going to have four kids I thought I'd better learn to cook. My other specialty is a chicken-and-rice casserole. And, of course, my famous tuna salad. Your fetish lesson will have to wait."

She set the bear on a window seat and slipped the bracelet on her wrist, twisting it to catch the light and hear its jingle. "Oh, I almost forgot—your Aunt Vivian called. Your service gave her my number. She sounded very nice, and I'm looking forward to meeting her. She said to . . ." Ashley took one look at Jed and trailed off. "Jed, what is it?"

"I usually call Viv in between assignments when I'm back in New York," he explained. "She never calls when I'm undercover." Too casually, he reached for the phone, punching in numbers.

Ashley shoved the hamburgers into the broiler and stuck a tray of frozen french fires into the microwave. She listened to Jed's side of the conversation—mostly terse "go on"s and "when?"s. Then there was a very long pause and a "Could you repeat that, Viv? Uh . . . repeat it again, please." And finally a weary "Unbelievable."

Jed hung up and raked both hands through his hair.

Giving him a moment to compose himself, Ashley sliced hamburger buns and took out a bottle of catsup. She stuck a fork into the hamburgers to see if they were done.

She wished she didn't have to ask the next question. "What's the bad news?"

"They've decided to begin the bone-marrow treatment soon," he said flatly. "It's a promising procedure using Father's own marrow, a high success rate for his type of . . . But, Ashley, there's more."

She turned around. Jed sank onto the couch, hands plowing through his thick chestnut hair a second time. "Ash, I can't believe . . ." He laughed harshly. "The thing is . . . Jeez, I think Aunt Viv is still in shock."

The pulse in Jed's jaw beat rapidly, and he expelled a breath in exasperation. "His timing stinks," he muttered.

"Tell me, Cooper."

He swallowed. "For eleven years the old man let me think I was dead to him. For eleven years, he's been too stubborn to let Viv even say my name out loud. And for eleven years, it seems he's been following my career. He's saved every magazine article. He even admitted to Viv that he talks about me to his friends—well, not his friends exactly, he doesn't have friends—but he talks to the partners about me. He confessed all this after the last set of X rays. Then he told Viv he wants . . ."

Jed looked up at her, and she felt sick. *It's not good to be too happy,* she reminded herself. *Don't ever trust anyone to make you too happy.*

"He wants you back in his life and back in the firm," she finished.

Jed nodded. "It's Father's way of extending an olive branch."

Ashley chewed on a nail, riding a wave of inexplicable fear. It was the fear she'd faced when her parents died, when the social worker took her away. The same fear that had overwhelmed her when Jed betrayed her five years ago.

"Maybe we've been taking it too fast, Jed," she babbled. "Maybe this is for the best. Your trip out East'll give us a chance to think. To reevaluate. Cool off and cut through the hormones. This has all been happening so fast. . . ."

Jed was off the couch and grabbing her arms so suddenly that she flinched.

"You fool! Do you think I'd let go of everything we talked about just like that? Didn't what I said about us, about following my dreams here in Chicago, mean anything to you?"

She bit her lip. "I can't stand between you and your father, Jed. I could never live with myself. And I won't ask you to make a choice between us."

Agitated, Ashley waved the open catsup bottle and drops splashed onto Jed's black T-shirt. "You have to go to him."

His jaw tightened. In a voice so low and hoarse she had to strain to hear, he said, "Ashley, honey, I don't know why, but I think you're deliberately creating problems for us. I can reconcile with my father and still come back here to you. It would've been easier after we were married, but I can try. And if it doesn't work, I'll still have you. Only the scenario's changed, not *us*."

He tipped up her chin. "Please say you believe me. You've got to trust me sometime. Do it now."

"We'll see. We'll see," she said, feeling her fear controlling her. She didn't even know what she was saying or why. "I don't think you realize what it's going to be like when you see your father. This is exactly what you've wanted since you first heard your father was sick. Can't you see? Everything's changed."

Ashley looked away, rocked by the bleakness of Jed's eyes. She couldn't believe she was sending him away! She couldn't believe she couldn't stop herself! She seemed to have divided into two Ashleys—one watching helplessly as the other destroyed them both.

"Anyway, dinner's ready," she said dully. "We still have to eat. Sit down and tell me about the two suspects and Harold."

His mouth as dry as dust, Jed sat and told her about his day, wondering what the hell was going on inside her gorgeous head. There was more to this than his father. And that was all he knew.

10

JED BUNCHED his napkin into a ball and tossed it on the kitchen table. "I'm going for a walk."

He hesitated, hoping Ashley would ask him to stay. He needed answers, dammit! But all he got was a small nod as he walked to the door.

He waved at the bodyguard, who was slouched on the lobby bench with a thermos of coffee, two paperbacks and three crossword-puzzle books. "Keep an eye on her, Callahan."

Shoving his hands in his pockets, Jed ate up the sidewalk in long strides. For such a beautiful warm autumn evening, he felt like crap.

He headed east, though he had no destination in mind. Eventually he found himself going toward the Lincoln Park Zoo, blindly passing a stream of joggers, walkers, bikers and in-line skaters. A biker swerved sharply to avoid him, cursing loudly. As calmly as a sleepwalker, Jed continued on, not even blinking at the close call. "She does love you," he muttered under his breath.

"Save the apology, buddy," the cyclist jeered.

Jed walked into the zoo, near closing hour, his shoes crunching on an overlay of peanut shells. He stopped in front of the lion exhibit.

He gritted his teeth. If she loved him, why was she using that phone call as an excuse to push him away?

Jed dropped onto a bench, the wind ruffling his hair. He stared at the big cats without seeing a thing.

ASHLEY TRIED to wash the dinner dishes. The problem was she kept scrubbing the same dish over and over.

She sighed, gnawing at a soapy nail. All she could see was Jed's bleak expression when he'd closed the door behind him. The days when she could protect herself by summoning up the cool controlled Ashley Jamieson were long gone, it seemed. She was seething with emotions, not one of which was cool or controlled.

"I'm going nuts," she finally said to Dusty.

The kitten merely pounced on a felt mouse.

"I have to get out of here or I'll end up discussing my love life with a cat," Ashley moaned.

She turned off the faucet and left the dishes in the sink. Hurrying into the bedroom, she tugged on a pair of leggings and a nutmeg pullover. Then she grabbed her shoulder bag and left. She got as far as the bodyguard in the lobby, a burly man who looked like the quintessential Irish cop. He walked outside with her, barring her way once they got to the top of the stone steps.

"Miss Jamieson, you're not to go anywhere unescorted. I saw Mr. Wyatt head east about forty-five minutes ago. Do you want me to walk with you?"

Ashley shook her head, her heart pounding. She felt a desperate need to take a long walk—alone.

She glanced at her watch. "Why, I'm surprised Jed didn't mention that I'm supposed to meet him at the store, officer—" she pointed "—just around the corner from all that construction."

She laughed, drawing the guard into her confidence. "Jed hates what he calls my rabbit food. I think he's going to load the shopping cart with steaks and potato chips."

Callahan crossed his arms over his broad chest, smiling. "Okay, Miss Jamieson, go ahead. I'll take care of things here."

She waved and walked quickly to the store. She ducked in and then right out again amidst a group of giggling teenagers.

Free at last, she walked block after block, the faint scent of burning leaves hanging in the air. Finally she forced herself to face the questions that had been nagging her. Why had she been so afraid when she heard the news about Jed's father? Why had that fear driven her to order Jed to go back to New York—for good and without her?

And she knew the answer. It had nothing to do with Jed's father, and everything to do with her. *You're a control freak, Jamieson. You're trying to abandon Jed before he abandons you! Because deep inside, you're terrified that's what he's going to do. If not this time, another time. The people you love always leave.*

Ashley blinked, squeezing back tears, thinking of the stark disappointment in Jed's eyes. Dammit, she wasn't going to give up the best thing that had ever happened to her because she was afraid! She couldn't run and hide at the first challenge to their relationship. They'd work things out. She'd follow him to New York. No one was leaving anyone!

Ashley was so mad at herself she kicked the base of a wire garbage container, stubbing her toe. "Dammit!"

Hopping, she headed back to the brownstone. She prayed it wasn't too late to make Jed understand. He must think—God only knew what he must think. She realized she just needed to *hear* Cooper say he'd never leave her.

Ashley started to run, almost tripping over a toy poodle a woman was walking. She needed Jed so bad it hurt.

She was so self-absorbed she didn't hear her name being called until she got past the heavy construction at the end of her block.

"Ashley!"

She whipped her head around, hoping it was Jed. It was Harold Bates, awkwardly carrying a casserole dish.

"Ashley. . ." he panted, the breeze threading his thin brown hair into boyish bangs. "Wait a minute." He took a gasp of air, as if he'd run a long distance. "Lucky I found you outside. I was going to ring your bell and ask you to come for a ride so we can discuss . . . dates and things. I'm not feeling well. Mother baked you these brownies—her secret recipe." He wheezed. "My inhaler's in my car. Asthma. Here . . ."

She took the brownies and followed him, concerned. She hadn't known Harold had asthma.

She slipped into the passenger side of Harold's Oldsmobile, closing the door to keep the dust from filtering in. Harold shut his door, too, and then he reached into the glove compartment for his inhaler.

ON HIS WAY back from the zoo, Jed stopped dead at the scene unfolding in front of him. Ashley had just climbed into a big white Oldsmobile with Harold. A surge of adrenaline accelerated his heartbeat as pieces of the puzzle fell into place with a sickening thud.

Nice, normal Harold Bates. The bumbler. The unassuming guy with an allergy problem that made him sneeze. Just like the flower delivery man. Just like the UPS client with the metronomes. The little guy who said there was only *one woman* besides Mother he'd ever felt comfortable with. *Amanda*.

Harold was the stalker!

Helplessly Jed told himself not to take a chance on spooking Harold into doing something rash. He might have a weapon.

Jed sucked in a breath and he analyzed his options. His .32 Smith & Wesson was in his duffel. A great little gun, weighing less than a pound. And right now as useless as dirt. His car, along with car phone, was parked two blocks away. Even his ID and wallet were upstairs.

For a few panicky seconds, Jed's mind shut down, overriding all his training. But then instinct took over. If Harold was going to drive someplace, Jed needed a car, and fast.

His eyes settled on an old blue Chevy, which had its windows down. Perfect. An old model could be hot-wired without smashing the steering column.

Grateful for the diversion of the construction crew, Jed turned into a car thief. He worked quickly, dexterous fingers remembering what they'd done a few times before. Nervously he raised his head to check on Harold and Ashley, still parked in a conservative white boat of a car. What the hell was Harold planning?

His heart wanted to vault through his rib cage when he heard the Olds rev up at a break in the drilling. Then the wires sparked, and the Chevy started. Jed put the car into gear and tailed Harold at a discreet distance, peering at the gas gauge and thanking whatever gods were at work that he had a full tank.

"BUCKLE YOUR SEAT BELT," Harold demanded, driving carefully through city traffic at a steady twenty-five miles an hour. He punched down the master lock for the windows and doors.

"Harold, what are you...?"

"You still don't get it, do you?" He waved what Ashley had thought was an inhaler at her.

Ashley's eyes widened. A gun! Harold had a gun!

Harold shoved the gun in her ribs, laughing at her gasp. "Now you have to do what I say. And I say put on your seat belt."

She stared at him openmouthed, wondering if this was a gag. Suddenly Harold slammed on the brakes, practically sending her head through the windshield. Dazed, Ashley calmly watched as Harold jerked a pair of handcuffs out of his pocket,

snagging her wrist to the passenger door's armrest.
Then he buckled her seat belt.

Still in a fog, she jerked her hand against the cuff.
And then she finally understood.

Harold was the stalker.

"Harold..." Ashley blinked back tears, determined to stay in control. As long as she could.
"Why?" she asked, her mouth dry. "Why?"

Harold sniffed and blinked, wiping at his watery eyes with a knuckle. "I should think that's obvious, matchmaker. Amanda was the love of my life. For two glorious months. Then you started fooling with her mind. You filled her head with visions of handsome virile men."

She choked back a sob. "No, Harold, I never—"

He waved the pistol in the air. "Shut up! I'm telling you I know Amanda would *never, ever,* leave me on her own. Amanda was very special. She was my first..." A dull flush crept up Harold's neck. "Well, Amanda and I had a very special intimacy, Ashley. With other girls, I could never... It's all been destroyed because of you."

He swung off Fullerton Avenue onto the Kennedy Expressway, not talking again until they merged onto I-94, heading north.

Harold settled back into his seat, going a steady fifty miles an hour. "Now, what was I saying? Oh, yes, my life destroyed. Even Mother couldn't fix things for me."

He giggled. "Amanda will finally appreciate how much I really love her when I tell her what I've done to you, though. And then she'll come back to me. Remember my poem?

Hickory dickory dock
Ashley ran up the clock
The clock struck one
And knocked her down
Hickory dickory red
Looks like Ashley's dead

"Now, no more questions until we're out of the city. A person could get killed in this traffic!"

He was insane!

Ashley bit her lower lip until it stung. She leaned her head back and closed her eyes, indulging in a spurt of self-pity. Now she'd never have the chance to make things right with Jed. Never have the chance to hear him say he wouldn't leave her.

An hour later, the city well behind them, Ashley moistened her lips and braved a question. "Where are you taking me, Harold?"

"Door County," Harold said easily, the sprawling lights of Milwaukee gradually coming into view. He turned a benign smile on her. "That area of Wisconsin they call the Cape Cod of the Midwest. Jam-packed in the summer with tourists, but by the fall it's very quiet. Mother and I have a lovely home there. It was Father's gift to her before he died."

She swallowed, struggling for control. "Why Door County, Harold? Why—"

"Why not kill you here, you mean?" he finished affably. "No, Ashley, I have to do this in a way that nothing can ever be proved. Only Amanda will know, and she'll never tell. Everyone else, including your P.I. friend, will see it as suicide."

He laughed at her gasp. "You see, all the notes and calls and gifts obviously drove you to the brink, Ashley. In fact, I watched the drama unfold in the lens of my telescope just like in *Rear Window*. Except I didn't witness a murder like James Stewart, I *planned* it! With the help of my partner Miss Stabe. I do like anagrams, don't you?"

He chuckled. "This is the script. You're distraught. You drive to Door County and you take a fatal fall, just like several of my poems prophesied. Of course, you'll leave a suicide note, too. I'll be the last person to have seen you alive. I'll tell everyone that when I gave you Mother's brownies you looked very agitated."

Ashley turned to him, eyes wide. "My car's still in Chicago."

"So what? I'll go back and drive your car up here. I'll even disguise myself as a nervous redhead and stop at a gas station to make sure I'm seen. I can be a very attractive woman, you know. I used to try on Mother's clothes and high heels when I was young." The little man shivered. "Until Father caught me and beat me with his belt."

Harold's face crumbled, and he was silent for a few minutes. Then he continued politely, "You won't mind my looking through your purse for your car keys and gas credit cards, will you? So good of you to bring it on your walk."

Ashley pulled at the cuff around her wrist. "Amanda will never love you because of what you've done, Harold. Never. She'll report you to the police and run for her life. You're a sick man!" She choked on a sob.

"Shut up!" Harold backhanded her across the face. "Amanda will love me, and she'll accept my proposal of marriage! Now shut up and don't make me act like Father."

While she stared at him incredulously, Harold slipped a Johnny Mathis tape into the tape deck and hummed along.

JED SETTLED BACK into the seat, his hands so tight on the steering wheel he had to consciously uncurl them. They were an hour past Milwaukee and still driving into the horizon, Lake Michigan a dark glassy gleam on their right. For hours, they'd driven through one rural Wisconsin town after another. Past Sheboygan, Manitowoc, Kewaunee.

It wasn't until Jed saw the sign for Sturgeon Bay that he made the connection and remembered Door County. He'd been here a long time ago—the summer he worked in Chicago after graduation.

Door County was a well-kept assembly of picture-perfect villages lined with beautiful beds of flowers. You could fish, sail, hike and shop. And explore the cliffs that lined Lake Michigan's shore.

Sick at heart, Jed remembered the poem.

March to the right
March to the left
March off a cliff
Right to your death

Exploding with a string of curses, Jed wondered if Ashley thought she was all alone.

He stubbed out a cigarette in the ashtray. "That's the one thing you have on you," he accused, "a freaking pack of cigarettes."

The muscle in his cheek jumped. He hadn't found Ashley again only to lose her. Not as long as he was alive to do something about it.

11

THE OLDS SWUNG onto an isolated back road. Its headlights illuminated a wooded area. The kind of forest, Ashley imagined, where wolves gobbled up children and witches cast spells on princesses.

She shuddered. She was tired, thirsty and terrified. The metal cuff bit into her flesh, and she twisted her wrist for the hundredth time. What must Jed think had happened to her?

At the metallic clink, Harold glanced at her. "We're almost there, Ashley. All this is ours, Mother's and mine." He waved a hand at the shadowy forest surrounding them, dark shapes looming like goblins.

"We're on the edge of Peninsula State Park here," he said proudly. "In fact, we have most of the trees and flowers in the park. Paper birch to sugar maples. Common ragweed—" Harold sneezed "—to wild strawberry and basil. When we take our hike to the cliffs tomorrow morning I'll show you everything."

She tried to still her quivering lips. "You're going to . . . uh, show me around, Harold?"

"Why, of course. I don't see why we can't be friends. I'm not a monster, Ashley." He looked genuinely hurt. "I'm a nice guy."

She gave a hysterical little laugh. "Nice guys don't kidnap people and force them to jump off cliffs!" She squeezed her eyes shut and reminded herself she was trying to reason with a madman.

"Ashley, really, I want us to be friends. I drove up last week and stocked the kitchen with food and wood for the fireplace. You'll love it. Amanda always did. There, isn't it something? Protected with a very sophisticated security system, too."

The car's headlights illuminated a long gravel driveway. Wheels crunching, Harold pulled in front of a sprawling ranch house. The perfect country retreat, all rustic white stone and picture windows and flower boxes.

Harold leaned toward Ashley, spaniel eyes imploring her to approve. He punched open the door locks and took the gun out of his pocket, then put it down in the recessed compartment housing the gearshift. "Come on, a truce, okay? We'll be friends?"

Ashley shrank back from him, her gaze darting frantically about her. She eyed the gun, then forced herself to look away. "No! I will not be friends with you! You want to kill me! You're crazy. Crazy!"

Desperate, she scratched his face with her free hand and then grabbed for the gun.

Harold fought her, knocking the pistol under the car seat.

Frantically Ashley leaned down and groped for it. Harold beat her to it, then sat up and put his palm to his cheek. "You hurt me, Ashley," he gasped. "That wasn't nice! And don't ever call me crazy again!"

She was breathing hard now, her self-pity and fear burned away. "Crazy, crazy, crazy," she chanted. "Don't think I'll write a suicide note, either! Maybe you'll kill me, but everyone'll know it was murder, Harold. You'll spend the rest of your life in jail!"

Harold grinned boyishly, the house's bright security lights casting his face with a garish glow. "Ashley, let me enlighten you."

Harold got out and stalked to Ashley's side of the car. He jerked the door open, and since she was still handcuffed to the armrest, she was yanked sideways and fell awkwardly to the damp leafy ground. He grabbed her thick hair, his grip surprisingly strong.

"Number one, you will write that note tomorrow morning before we visit the cliffs." Harold relaxed his grip and patted her head. "I don't like blood, Ashley. Did you notice how the canary was killed? I twisted its neck—" he tapped the gun on Ashley's throat "—all the way around, like the cap on a jelly jar. And Smoky's not even dead—I gave him to Mother. I'm such a good son...."

"Go to hell," she gasped, wrenching her hair free and futilely yanking her hand against the cuff.

"No, you have it wrong. *You're* the one going to hell—tomorrow." Harold sniffed and wiped his nose. "We really must get out of the night air. My allergies you know. But first, let's resolve our differences. Tell me you'll write the note, so I won't have to hurt you. Then tell me you'll be my friend."

She took a deep breath, feeling the cold air play over her skin, drawing goose bumps. "I'll write the note."

"And we'll be friends," Harold prompted.

"We'll be friends," Ashley said, crossing her fingers behind a tuft of grass and imagining spitting in his face.

JED LEANED against a solid white pine and sucked in a breath, every muscle singing out for action. He'd never wanted to kill a man before. Even when he'd nailed the baby-sellers on his last assignment, he'd been clearheaded, cool, controlled. But seeing Harold torment Ashley, he was consumed with rage.

He wiped a trembling wrist across his damp forehead. He'd never been trained for a hostage situation. Although he had attended one class on crisis scenario's at the training center in Alabama. He remembered the lecturer dryly talking about barricades, stun grenades, flash protection, ballistic armor, UHF radios and wall-rappelling equipment.

Jed clenched his jaw until it hurt. Unfortunately the only weapon he had was himself. He forced himself to take slow deep breaths.

He'd left the car at the end of the private driveway and crept up the trail, using the thick stand of trees as cover. He was situated just beyond the clearing outside the house, and he'd heard enough to know Harold was on the edge. The house was undoubtedly equipped with a high-tech security system. Any break-in later that night would be less than subtle.

He could see Harold unlocking the handcuffs and pulling Ashley toward the house. Hunkering down under the pine, he heard Harold mention tomorrow. So Ashley was probably safe till then. But there was always the chance that Harold would make his move earlier, so Jed didn't dare go for help.

Harold seemed obsessed with the cliffs. If Harold took her there, Jed would be able to nail him without tripping the alarm. Jed groaned, raking a hand through his hair. He had no choice but to wait under the goddamn tree until morning. Scraping together some pine needles, he made a pillow and sighed. It was going to be a long night.

HAROLD DRAGGED her inside.

"Ashley," he said eagerly, "I can't wait to show you the house. And wait till you see what I did to surprise Amanda."

With a great effort, Ashley spoke, amazed that her voice sounded normal. "Okay, Harold. Whatever you say."

Harold bustled them through the all-wood home. Rustic open beams and supports ran through a huge room. Proudly he pointed out the mounted fish covering one enormous wall. "Father was a great fisherman. Those trophies are from all over the country. Mountain trout here, big-mouth bass there."

He posed in front of a glass cabinet. "This is Father's prized gun collection. And every animal head on that wall was shot by Father."

Filled with revulsion, Ashley eyed the wall opposite the fish. It was covered by elk, deer, moose and bear heads.

She tried not to shiver as Harold led her through the great room. Then he tugged her into the master bedroom. Ashley noted the skylights which would fill the vaulted room with sunlight during the day. A high canopy bed took up the center of the room. She told herself if it wasn't for the fact that Harold was going to murder her, she could pity his desperate desire to please.

"This is my surprise," he said eagerly. "The bedroom. I worked with an architect to plan it. And I built a small gym for Amanda to work out in, too. I ordered *all* the latest equipment. Do you think she'll like it?"

Ashley bit her lip and swallowed. "It's . . . it's lovely, Harold," she croaked. "You did this all for Amanda?"

"Yes, all for her. This is where we'll honeymoon. That's what you're going to help me with later, Ashley. Wedding plans." He looked into her face. "But I can see you're tired. Would you like some hot chocolate? A glass of sherry? We can do the plans tomorrow morning if you'd prefer."

Ashley eyed the gun in Harold's hand and nodded. "Actually, Harold, I think I'd just like to go to sleep now."

She spent a fitful night locked in a guest bedroom with boarded-over windows. She didn't sleep for more than twenty minutes at a time. Harold had thoughtfully provided her with a nightshirt, toothpaste, toothbrush and herbal-scented shampoo.

Ashley woke up bone weary and depressed. There would be no reprieve. Not unless Harold dropped dead. And he seemed horribly healthy. *What was Jed thinking?* Angrily she wiped away the tears running down her cheeks.

Before breakfast, Harold forced Ashley to look through bridal magazines. She turned page after glossy page of brides in frothy white concoctions, helping him choose Amanda's gown. And then she looked at pictures of homes. Harold had stacks of magazines full of dream houses—Tudors, colonials, Georgians, ranch and Spanish haciendas. She feigned interest, anything to buy herself time to come up with a plan. Any plan!

Harold beamed at Ashley's inane noises of approval. "I think white-on-white china and Waterford crystal, don't you, Ashley?"

Harold was wearing an electric blue jogging outfit, and his hair was neatly slicked to the side with a knife-edged part. He looked about as dangerous as a turtle.

"Yes." Her voice quavered. "Certainly. That's very. . . very Amanda."

He cuffed Ashley to a kitchen chair and happily dictated a suicide note, which she wrote. While he spoke, Harold scrambled eggs, made coffee, toast and bacon, and mixed a blueberry muffin batter from scratch. Still not believing this was happening, Ashley felt like throwing up at the rich aroma of breakfast. She ate just enough to please Harold.

After tidying the kitchen, Harold sealed the note in a scented pink envelope, then marched her outside into the crisp sunlight, the gun at her back.

He breathed in noisily and stretched vigorously. "Ah, smell that fresh country air."

Ashley swallowed. And then she remembered what Jed had told her what seemed like a million years ago, when he'd advised her on how to protect herself against an assailant.

Saying a little prayer, Ashley gathered all her strength and kneed Harold right between the legs.

"Umph!" Harold clutched himself, tears streaming down his face.

Ashley spun and ran, galloping straight into the national forest behind the house.

Retching weakly, Harold tottered after her.

Within minutes, she was flying down a wide unmarked trail. She could hear only her own panting. She paused, desperately looking for a detour to confuse Harold.

She stopped at a path marked with a sign for the Eagle Trail Cliffs. Frantically she told herself it would be perfect.

Ashley's hair snagged on a dogwood branch at the path's turn. She wrenched free, not noticing the few russet hairs that remained behind, fluttering like a flag.

The forest was deserted. No birds sang. No animals rustled. The trail was becoming steeper, narrower. After fifteen minutes she was climbing and scrambling over a series of thick exposed roots. The forest embraced her, the trees an autumn fire of burnished apricot, lemon and cranberry.

After an exhausting hour, Ashley found herself creeping along a high bluff. To her right, she could see Green Bay, a long drop down craggy cliffs. The drop Harold wanted her to take.

She halted at a fork in the pathway, catching her breath. One looping sliver of a trail doubled over and over, flowing up with each curve. It ended at a row of caves on top of the highest dolomite cliff. The other path jutted out over the bay, rimming its twisting curves.

Saying a little prayer, Ashley took the path to the caves. A hideout, she told herself, until dark. Then she'd find her way back down to civilization, by touch, if necessary. There was no way Harold would find her up there!

She crept carefully now, climbing higher and higher onto the narrow rope of trail. It became so steep and twisted she finally dropped to her hands and knees, not trusting her balance.

She crawled the last few yards and hauled herself up over the cliff's edge into a stand of trees. She caught her breath and stepped gingerly into a clearing facing the caves. She looked down only once at the glimmering bay, shaken by the sight of the sheer vertical drop.

Panting, Ashley picked her way carefully across the steep ground, blanketed with loose pebbles and stones. She ducked into a misshapen opening. Dead tired, she rested, knees hunched up to her chin.

BREATHING HARD, Jed took cover behind a towering spruce. It was as far as he could go without stepping into the open where the caves were.

He'd been up with the sun. He'd cheered silently when Ashley had kneed Harold. And then he'd watched fearfully as Harold tracked Ashley like an Indian scout. The little man's progress had been slow, but he'd gained strength and speed toward the end—and he'd continually fingered his pistol.

Jed's lips flattened into a grim line. This scout didn't know that his prey had a guardian angel.

Jed held his breath as Harold crept boldly into the clearing, his nose twitching like a rabbit's. He wiped his forehead with his forearm. It was cool and he'd damn near frozen during the night, covering himself with an ineffectual blanket of pine needles. But now he was sweating with fear.

"COME OUT, come out, wherever you are," Harold chanted.

Ashley's heart plummeted. He'd found her! She felt as if she was in a bad horror movie, the kind where the villain gets burned, buried and drowned, but never goes away.

She sobbed once, then rested her head against the dry earth wall, torn with indecision. If she faced him one on one, Harold would surely kill her, for he had the gun. But if she stayed put, he would find her, anyway. He was obviously intent on a relentless cave-by-cave search.

Ashley dug her nails into her palms.

Don't panic, Jamieson. Take control of the situation. You've got to stay alive. For Jed.

And then she had an idea.

Steadying her nervous fingers, she reached for a stone and flung it over the cliff. It tumbled for ages, just the way her body would if Harold had his way. Then she picked up a large sharp rock and stood flattened behind the cave entrance, silently daring Harold to find her.

Harold froze at the sound of the falling stone. After a moment he put both hands on his hips and shrieked, "Now, Ashley, this is *my* game, and we have to play by *my* rules. And—"

Adrenaline pumping, Jed sprang onto Harold's back. They crashed down the sloping ground, stopping at the very edge of the precipice. The pistol flew out of Harold's hand, landing in a fat clump of Queen Anne's lace.

Jed locked his hands around Harold's throat.

The little man squeaked for breath. But he managed to grab a small flat rock and swing it against Jed's head with all his strength.

Jed saw whole constellations before his eyes. He toppled to the side, his momentum carrying his shoulders over the edge of the cliff. Vaguely he heard Ashley scream somewhere in the distance as the rest of his body started to roll over the ledge, a dizzy slow-motion ride to oblivion.

No!

With one last desperate move, Jed twisted his body around and grabbed for the low-hanging branch of an ironwood. Scrambling onto the cliff edge, Jed righted himself.

Harold stamped in frustration. "No fair!" he yelled. "No . . ." Harold slipped on the loose stones underfoot. Arms flapping, off balance, he slid down the incline, his feet dancing on the stones like someone in a log-rolling contest.

"Nooo! Not meee!" With a piercing scream, Harold skated off the cliff.

Jed extended a hand toward Harold, then watched in horror as the flailing hand missed his by inches.

Harold's shrieks split the cool morning air as he fell, until he hit the shore, finally silent.

12

JED HAULED Ashley up hard against his chest. They bent their heads, staring at the broken figure lapped at by Green Bay's gentle waves.

"You have the gun," Jed said inanely.

"I got it when you and Harold were trying to kill each other," she told him, panting. "I thought you might need a friend." She gave an extremely shaky laugh. She knew if she didn't laugh she'd cry and never stop.

"How did you get here?" she cried. Then she blurted out, "I love you."

"I love you, too. I followed you from Chicago. And I promise he won't bother you again."

Jed framed her face with his hands and nuzzled her lips, her cheeks, her eyes, as if he couldn't get enough of her. "Listen up good. If you didn't know this before, you're gonna know it now. I'm *never* going to leave you, honey. Not for New York or for ten fathers and six mothers. Even if you sic a rottweiler on me."

Ashley forgot Harold. She forgot she was standing on top of a cliff. Once, she'd thought she needed to hear Jed say those magic words. But not anymore. Some things didn't need to be said.

She wiped away a tear. "Cooper—" she gulped "—I was a fool for ever doubting you. And if you'll forgive me, I, um...well, I've always wanted to be a September bride."

"This isn't a trick? You're not gonna try and ship me back to New York?" Jed eyed her suspiciously. "'Cause it won't work, you know."

"I know. I finally know a lot of things. Now kiss me senseless, counselor."

He did.

Epilogue

JED CIRCLED the bedroom yet again. "God, Cooper, you don't believe in doing things by halves, do you? Why does mine always cry more?" He studied the baby in his arms, finally satisfied that her cries had diminished into contented gurgles. He was sure she was smiling at him.

"It was your idea, remember? Four little girls? This is only the first installment." Ashley rocked the sleepy baby in her arms.

Jed appraised his wife with a lazy look. "It wasn't exactly *all* my idea." Jed's lips quirked. "The twin part, I mean. As I recall, you dreamed that up. Remember?"

Ashley ducked her head, remembering that particular time very well indeed.

She studied her daughter and remembered another time, too. A little before the twins were conceived, about a year ago, there'd been a moment in her life when everything had seemed wrong—when she'd wished she'd slip over the rainbow and wake up in a brand-new world. And, by God, she had!

She was over the rainbow, and the view was spectacular.

"You there, hon?"

Ashley lifted her head, a secret smile playing on her lips. "Well, we needed twins," she said defensively. "A Sara for your mother and a Suzanne for mine." She smiled down at Sara. "Your father said Sara looks just like your mother, except for the hair."

Carefully holding a sleepy Suzanne, Jed sat at the edge of the toy-box bench next to Ashley. He nipped his wife's neck playfully. "Thanks for putting up with Father's visit. I mean, I know you didn't need him underfoot while I was at the office."

"You know how proud I am of your work—and so is your father."

Jed chuckled. "I don't know about that. I don't think my child-advocate work exactly excites him."

Jed imitated his father's gruff voice in a whisper, so as not to wake the girls. "'I don't pretend to begin to understand the lure of this kind of work, but if that's what makes you happy, son...'" Jed's voice trailed off, and he shot Ashley a wry look.

"Jed, that was almost a year ago. And you had so many other things to settle between you then. It takes time."

Ashley put Sara in one crib and Jed put Suzanne in another, each with identical mobiles and bumper pads.

"Your father and I got to know each other really well this last visit, Jed. And he *is* proud of you. One day he'll tell you so himself."

Jed nodded. "Maybe you're right. I guess it's amazing we've come this far. He *has* changed."

Jed put his hands on Ashley's shoulders and pressed his forehead against hers. "Um, Jamie, to get back to our original subject, do you remember how we got these two kids of ours?"

Ashley threaded her hands up under Jed's T-shirt, feeling the crisp hairs curl under her fingers.

"Why don't you refresh my memory. I seem to recall we have to start in the living room—"

"—and finish in the bedroom." Jed glanced at the cribs. "How long do we have?"

Ashley grinned. "How long do you need?"

"You are so bad." Jed put his hand in Ashley's and led her into the family room. "C'mere." He patted the cushion next to him on the couch. "Let me tell you what I look for in a woman, so you can make me a match."

Ashley shook her head. "No, let me tell you, counselor. Let me whisper my preferences in your ear and you can make *me* a match." She leaned over and whispered in Jed's ear. She blew each word out softly, teasing him beyond reason.

And then he found her the perfect match, wickedly satisfying her every preference, and then some.

HARLEQUIN®

Temptation®

IS TEN!

Join the festivities as Harlequin celebrates
Temptation's tenth anniversary in 1994!

Look for tempting treats from your favorite
Temptation authors all year long. The celebration
begins with Passion's Quest—four exciting sensual
stories featuring the most elemental passions....

The temptation continues with Lost Loves, a sizzling
miniseries about love lost...love found. And watch for
the 500th Temptation in July by bestselling author
Rita Clay Estrada, a seductive story in the vein
of the much-loved tale, THE IVORY KEY.

In May, look for details of an irresistible offer:
three classic Temptation novels by Rita Clay Estrada,
Glenda Sanders and Gina Wilkins in a collector's
hardcover edition—free with proof of purchase!

After ten tempting years, *nobody* can resist

Temptation®

Where do you find hot Texas nights, smooth Texas charm and dangerously sexy cowboys?

Crystal Creek reverberates with the exciting rhythm of Texas. Each story features the rugged individuals who live and love in the Lone Star state.

"...Crystal Creek wonderfully evokes the hot days and steamy nights of a small Texas community...impossible to put down until the last page is turned."
—*Romantic Times*

"...a series that should hook any romance reader. Outstanding."
—*Rendezvous*

"Altogether, it couldn't be better." —*Rendezvous*

Don't miss the next book in this exciting series.
SHAMELESS by SANDY STEEN

Available in July wherever Harlequin books are sold.

RIGHT MAN...WRONG TIME

Remember that one man who turned your world upside down. Who made you experience all the ecstatic highs of passion and lows of loss and regret. What if you met him again?

You dared to lose your heart once and had it broken. Dare you love again?

JoAnn Ross, Glenda Sanders, Rita Clay Estrada, Gina Wilkins and Carin Rafferty. Find their stories in Lost Loves, Temptation's newest miniseries, running May to September 1994.

In July, experience *Forms of Love* by Rita Clay Estrada, Book #500 from Temptation! Dan Lovejoy had lost his wife in a tragic accident—then he met her double. Only this woman who looked like Kendra wasn't Kendra. Moreover, she had some very *unusual* secrets of her own. Dan couldn't help himself—he started to fall in love with her. But who was he falling in love with? A moving, romantic story in the tradition of *The Ivory Key*.

What if...?

LOST3

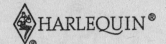

EXPECTATIONS
Shannon Waverly

Eternity, Massachusetts, is a town with something special going for it. According to legend, those who marry in Eternity's chapel are destined for a lifetime of happiness. As long as the legend holds true, couples will continue to flock here to marry and local businesses will thrive.

Unfortunately for the town, Marion and Geoffrey Kent are about to prove the legend wrong!

EXPECTATIONS, available in July from Harlequin Romance®, is the second book in Harlequin's new cross-line series, **WEDDINGS, INC.** Be sure to look for the third book, **WEDDING SONG,** by
Vicki Lewis Thompson (Harlequin Temptation® #502), coming in August.

WED-2